# THE GAME MASTER

PIERREDEN GLAVE

GIFTED QUILL PUBLISHING LLC

**The Game Master**

# CONTENTS

My dad used to tell me, "Be careful when you speak out loud to the universe; you never know what's listening."

# CHAPTER 1

# MOMENT OF TRUTH

I nside the lab of a small game development company in Seattle, Washington, Joshua Peters, a man in his early thirties with sandy brown hair, stood hunched over a table. His green eyes beamed with anticipation as he awaited testing their new creation. He stared at his friend and assistant, Lin Huang, a young, studious-looking man who was diligently typing on a keyboard.

"Well?" Joshua asked.

"It takes a full minute for it to upload to the game console. It's only halfway there," Lin replied.

Joshua began pacing back and forth, then paused and asked, "Did you remember to—" before Joshua could finish his question, Lin cut him off, answering, "Yes. I ran the integration and the build tests last night."

"Okay, cool."

"It's done," Lin said, pushing his glasses above the bridge of his nose.

"Great, let's do this!" Joshua exclaimed, eagerly grabbing the game controller and pressing the button on a silver, octagon-shaped device. The console turned on, making a soft humming noise while bright green, fluorescent lights filled its edges. He looked up at the large, wall-mounted TV as the camera lens at the center of the device rotated, scanning Joshua's tall six-foot frame. Afterwards, the screen displayed the face of a court jester, looking thin and pale, with a long, pointed chin and a nose that tapered to a point.

The court jester spoke in a monotone voice devoid of inflection and said, "Hello, Joshua. I am The Game Master. Would you like to play a game?"

"Yes, I would," Joshua answered.

"What game would you like to play?" The Game Master asked.

"How about Cosmic Space Blasters?"

"As you wish," The Game Master replied.

The image on the TV screen transitioned to an outer space motif. "Do you want me to explain the game to you?" The Game Master asked.

"No need, just play."

"Remember, you must get through each level in order to face the final boss, which is me, the Game Master," the court jester said.

"I know, let's play," Joshua replied, his impatience palpable.

Joshua's avatar appeared on the screen, dressed as an astronaut and armed with a polished laser weapon. He stood ready for battle. Suddenly, the Game Master's spaceship materialized in the sky and hovered over Joshua. He looked up at the craft and began powering up his rifle. Its door slid open, and a swarming horde of goblin winged creatures emerged, swooping down towards him, their teeth and talons sharp for the kill.

Joshua stepped back from the approaching monsters, firing his weapon in rapid succession, easily killing them. The room resonated with the sounds of laser blasts and explosions from the surrounding speakers as he obliterated the entire goblin fleet. The ashes of their disintegrated bodies rained onto the ground, forming a black mountainous pile, which he had to leap over to get to the next area of the game.

Joshua's fingers danced over the controller as he sped through the levels. Each monster fell before him, their roars of defeat echoing in his ears. Within twenty minutes, he had conquered every stage.

When he reached the last level, the scenery transformed into a desolate, arid planet. The ground was cracked and lifeless. The sky was dull gray. Joshua's avatar materialized, standing near the wreckage of a small aircraft. He was clad in a sleek silver metallic battle suit, a laser pistol clenched in his hand.

The Game Master appeared a few seconds later in gleaming green battle armor. In his hands, he held a futuristic, cannon-like weapon that hummed with deadly energy.

The two adversaries stood just five feet apart from one another, prepared for an epic showdown.

"You have reached the last level. Now, you must defeat me in order to be declared the winner. Are you ready?" The Game Master asked.

"Yes!" Joshua answered.

The Game Master began shooting energetic laser beams at Joshua, who skillfully used his rear thrusters to dodge each blast. Joshua fought back, propelling himself into the air, landing behind The Game Master. Swiftly, he fired his laser pistol, hitting critical areas along The Game Master's back and head, draining its health meter with every shot.

The Game Master changed tactics and began throwing a relentless stream of plasma grenades at Joshua's virtual character. One grenade detonated near Joshua and launched him backwards into the air. In an instant, Joshua recovered and dodged the next barrage of grenades that were flying towards him. With one hand, he precisely caught a grenade in mid-air and threw it back at him. The explosive impact caused The Game Master to meet its fiery end.

The screen faded to black, and the Game Master's face popped up and declared, "You have defeated me. You are now the Game Master." A triumphant melody began playing as the end credits glided across the screen.

Lin jumped up and down, shouting victoriously. "Yes, we did it! That was amazing!"

Joshua hurled the game controller against the wall, smashing it, and yelled, "No, no, no!"

"What's wrong?" Lin asked, surprised by Joshua's reaction to the game.

"The Game Master sounds like a robot. He's not interactive like I wanted, and it was way too easy. We need to increase the battle system's AI. The game must be able to counter every attack as if it doesn't want to lose. Make a player sweat," Joshua said as he walked to the nearest computer terminal and started typing.

"But we already integrated all possible codes and algorithms into the battle logic," Lin calmly explained.

"There has to be something more we can add to improve it," Joshua replied, still typing in frustration.

"Josh, you're one of the best gamers in the world. What's easy for you might be difficult for most people," Lin pointed out. When Joshua didn't respond, Lin asked in frustration, "Are you hinting at the idea of rewriting code and rebuilding everything? That's too much."

"All the greatest inventors faced tough challenges. It didn't stop them, and it won't stop me," Joshua confidently stated as he meticulously examined the code on the screen.

Lin, disappointed, gazed down at the floor and shook his head at the thought of starting over.

Joshua stopped typing, caught himself, and spoke in an apologetic tone. "I'm sorry, man. But I know we're onto something great if we can just get it right. I don't... I can't give up yet."

"It's okay, I understand, but it's going to be a lot of work," Lin said, his spirits deflated.

Joshua stood up from his chair and walked over to Lin, placed his hand on his shoulder, saying with sincerity, "You're a big help to me. I know we can do this." Joshua paused, glancing at his watch, before continuing, "It's getting late. Go home, eat some dinner, and get some rest. We'll get back at it in the morning. Greg and Susan will be here. We'll figure it out."

Before walking out of the lab, Lin nodded and said, "Okay, don't stay up too late. See you in the morning."

Joshua returned his attention to the computer and began running tests, gazing at countless lines of code. He rubbed his eyes, feeling a sense of mounting frustration. "Damn it!" He pounded his fist on the desk and shouted, "I'll give anything for this game to work the way I want! Anything! Anything!" his voice echoed throughout the empty lab.

Later that night, on a faintly lit road, Joshua drove home to a peaceful northeast suburb of Seattle. During the drive, he took a trip down memory lane, reflecting on his life and childhood. When he was young, he would sneak into the family room late at night and play video games while everyone else was asleep. He realized that as a young child, he had a natural talent for seamlessly mastering difficult video games and could easily defeat them during his first playthrough. He also recalled how his gaming addiction had put a financial strain on his middle-class family in California, where the cost of living was high. Olga, Joshua's mother, and Harold, his father, were both schoolteachers. They both worked tirelessly to provide for him and his older brother, Liam. Even work during summer breaks to earn extra money. But the added expense of buying video games and the latest gaming consoles for Joshua put a strain on the family's budget. Joshua found a solution by taking up a newspaper route before school and on weekends to cover his gaming expenses.

Around the same time he picked up his newspaper route, his parents started going through a bitter divorce. They separated when he was in junior high, and money continued to be an obstacle in his life. After high school, Joshua went on to college; he struggled to pay his way through Caltech and earned a degree in computer science and engineering. After his graduation ceremony, he told his mother and brother that he wanted to create his own video gaming platform that would blow all the other systems out of the water. His mother gave him a congratulatory hug, then patted him on his shoulder and told him to grow up and get a real job. He embraced his mother warmly and quietly dismissed her advice.

Joshua used his video gaming skills to create a successful career through online competitions and endorsements. He amassed a small fortune, became one of the top gamers in the world, and earned the illustrious title "The Josh." However, after many tournaments, his passion for playing video games diminished. He found the games were not challenging enough for him to continue playing or competing. But his new gaming system would change that.

After three years of painstaking work, all the while draining his bank account due to a lack of private funding, Joshua finally achieved his dream. With the help of his team, he had created their first game and platform on which to play it, called "The Game Master System." The Game Master was a new gaming console equipped with advanced AI logic that would intuitively provide its user with a more challenging and immersive gameplay, in accordance with their skill level. That was his hope anyway; his dream was all but shattered today at the lab by the game's lackluster performance. He knew he had to improve the AI in the gaming system in order for it to be a financial success. If he could accomplish that, it would also bring more respect to his name throughout the gaming community.

# CHAPTER 2

# HOME LIFE

"He's not home yet," Chloe said, peering out the front window of her home.

After they got engaged, the first thing she and Joshua did was buy a house. She wanted a sleek design, and he wanted something secluded with a large backyard, and this house was perfect. She paced back and forth across the living room.

"He should be home. It's almost nine o'clock. A man needs to protect his family," Mr. Shaw said over the phone.

He was old school, very rigid and orderly. Chloe shared his concerns, but she wasn't going to let him know that. He had been lecturing her like this for thirty years, and by now she knew just how to handle him.

"I'm safe, Dad," she replied. "The alarm system is on. Really, I'm fine."

Mr. Shaw continued in a disapproving tone, "He needs to stop chasing fantasies and get himself a real job and stop wasting all his money on that nonsensical endeavor."

"Dad, that's just how Josh is. He has a big imagination," she said defensively.

"Chloe, don't take this the wrong way. But I think you should reconsider your decision to marry him," Mr. Shaw firmly advised.

The lights of Joshua's pickup truck pulling into the driveway saved her from an uncomfortable conversation.

"Listen, Dad, he just got home. Love you. Talk to you later." Chloe hung up with a sigh of relief. Then, in a burst of energy, she rushed to sit on the couch and opened a book, pretending to be absorbed in her reading. Joshua walked in and shut the door as she sat there playing with her long, mousy brown hair, eyes buried in the pages before her—as if she was completely oblivious to him.

"Hey, babe!" he lovingly called out before hanging up his jacket and strolling into the living room.

"Oh, hi, sweetie. How was your day?" she asked, turning the pages of the book.

He looked curiously at her. "You don't want to know why I'm home late? I thought you would have been upset or worried," he said, setting his laptop down on the coffee table.

Without glancing at him, she continued to flip through the pages and responded nonchalantly, "You're busy at the studio. I get it."

"Oh, alright then," he said, shrugging his shoulders as he headed towards the kitchen.

She sprang up from the sofa and followed him, wrapping her arms tightly around him from behind. "Of course I was worried," she said affectionately.

Turning to face her, he leaned down as she stood on her toes, and they shared a passionate kiss.

"I love you so much, Josh," she whispered, nuzzling her head against his chest.

"I love you too, hon," he said, kissing her forehead.

As they released their embrace, he glanced at his watch.

"Two questions. What's for dinner and where's the kid?"

"Pizza from takeout and the kid is upstairs playing video games, as usual."

"You know, you should order a cookbook. I read in a marriage manual, when a man comes home to his castle, there should always be a warm full-course meal waiting for him," he said jokingly.

A smirk crossed her lips as she said, "Really? And I read husbands are supposed to be home before dark."

"Hmm, Touché. I'm going upstairs to check on the kid. It's almost past his bedtime," he said, turning to walk away.

She teased him with a pat on the rear. "You're a pain in the ass, but you sure got some nice buns."

Joshua smiled and brilliantly retorted. "You don't have a lack of junk in the trunk either, hot pants."

They both burst into laughter as he left the kitchen.

Kyle Peters, a 13-year-old with sandy brown hair, sat on the edge of his bed, absorbed in a video game. His fingers mashed the buttons on the controller while his blue-gray eyes remained fixed on the screen. He watched with anxiety as zombie-like creatures chased his digital character.

After the tragic car crash that claimed the lives of Joshua's brother Liam and sister-in-law Debbie six months ago, Joshua took guardianship of his nephew. Kyle was an only child and devastated by the loss of both his parents. He was very close to his dad, who would regularly take him fishing and out to different sports events. He missed those outings. And he missed his mom making his favorite dishes and teaching him how to play the guitar. Here in Seattle, he had no friends, nor did he want to make any. Instead, he tried to stay connected to old acquaintances he left in California, but the distance proved difficult to maintain. He now felt alone and had committed himself to escaping the cruelties of life by playing video games for hours after school.

There was a knock on the door. "Come in!" Kyle exclaimed as he pounded the buttons on his controller.

Joshua walked in. "How's it going, champ?"

"Not too good. I'm getting my ass kicked," Kyle answered, disgruntled, frantically pressing the buttons on the controller.

"Watch the potty mouth," Joshua said in a parental tone.

"Sorry, Uncle Josh."

"What are you playing?" Joshua asked.

"Zombie Killers."

"Ah yes, I remember that one. Pretty cool game," Joshua said with fondness.

"I'll never be as good as you, Uncle Josh."

Joshua sat on the bed next to him and said, "Remember what I taught you. A good gamer must be patient and learn the patterns. If you're outnumbered or facing an enemy stronger than you, just calm yourself and think."

"Oh no! I ran out of health packs!" Kyle shouted in a panic. "Damn, I'm out of ammo!" He stared hopelessly at the screen as his avatar became surrounded by vile, decomposing zombies that ripped into his flesh.

"Game Over" appeared on the screen.

Kyle flung the controller across the room in frustration, blurting out, "Stupid game!"

"Whoa, take it easy, buddy. Are you okay? What's going on?" Joshua asked, eyeing him with concern.

Though Joshua paid for weekly therapy sessions to help Kyle with grieving and socialization, he would brush off their advice and deal with his problems on his own. He was a lot like his uncle in that way. Kyle looked down at the floor, trying to hide the tear running down his face, saying, "Uncle Josh, I miss them. I miss them so much."

"So do I, all of them," Joshua said, hugging his nephew tightly, "but you'll always have me."

Joshua, who lost both his parents a few years ago and now his older brother, fully understood his nephew's experience of loneliness and sorrow that always seemed to creep in at the worst moments.

# CHAPTER 3

# NOT MARKET READY

The next morning, Joshua and his team focused on training the AI in the Game Master System to improve it. They sat at their desks, immersed in their tasks. Gregory Bernard, a young African American man in his late twenties, was the audio engineer and character designer. He wore headphones as he analyzed the characters on the screen.

Susan Fisher, a young woman in her mid-twenties with blonde hair, sat across from Gregory. Her blue eyes fixated on her screen, taking sips of coffee as she reviewed still background shots and searched for ways to refine the game's 3-D graphics.

Lin, Gregory, and Susan thought the system was ready for sale, but Joshua had a different view. Instead, his frustration grew, and he pushed his team even more to achieve his goal.

Joshua steadily shifted his focus from spending time with his family at home to spending more time in the lab, where he constantly evaluated, upgraded, and played The Game Master.

Later that afternoon, Joshua stepped out of the studio to grab some supplies. As he did, two young, energetic online gamers spotted him and made their way over. "Hey, it's The Josh!" exclaimed a young man with fiery red hair as he approached Joshua with a microphone in hand. Walking beside him was a tall young man sporting a rock and roll t-shirt and black ripped jeans, holding a video camera.

"Morning, Mr. Peters. Can you give a quick interview to two of your biggest fans for our podcast? Please," the young man with red hair asked, practically begging, as he rolled up the sleeve on his plaid shirt.

"Sure, fellas. Why not?" Joshua answered.

"Awesome!" the tall man said with excitement.

"What's your names?" Joshua asked.

"I'm Paul," the redheaded young man replied, then pointed at his friend. "And that's Tony. "

"Nice to meet you both. What's the name of your podcast?" Joshua inquired, folding his arms.

"Games, Gamers, and More Games," Tony answered, holding up the camera.

"You got two minutes. Let's do this," Joshua stated.

Tony and Paul high-fived each other. Paul stood next to Joshua. Tony began filming: "Three, two, one."

"We're here today talking to world champion gamer Joshua Peters, better known as The Josh!" Joshua gave the thumbs up and waved. Paul continued. "So, what's going on with the new top-secret development project we read about online? You said it's been three years in the making. It must be something really cool."

"That's true, but I can't give too many details. All I can say is that our team is trying to create something unique, challenging, and affordable for all gamers worldwide," Joshua answered with enthusiasm.

"What's the holdup? We've all been waiting for it to come out," Tony asked while zooming in on Joshua's face.

"Like I mentioned, I can't go into details, but our team has made impressive advancements. Unfortunately, we're currently facing issues in training the AI to my desired level, and that's all I can say for now. Take care, guys," Joshua said as he headed towards his pickup truck.

"Aww, come on, is that all you can tell us?" Paul asked, expressing disappointment.

"Sorry, guys," Joshua said, putting his hand on the truck door.

"Can you sign my t-shirt, Josh?" Paul asked with deference.

Joshua smiled. "Sure, why not?"

Tony handed Joshua a black marker. Joshua signed the t-shirt on the hood of his truck and gave it back to Paul. Then he got into his pickup, waved, and drove away.

Paul stood in front of the camera, holding his freshly autographed T-shirt, and announced, "This is Games, Gamers, and More Games signing off."

The brief video interview created quite a stir within the online gaming community, captivating millions around the globe and piquing the interest of an elderly gentleman living in Geneva, Switzerland.

# CHAPTER 4

# THE IMPOSSIBLE DREAM

Two weeks after unsuccessful attempts at improving the battle system's AI to Joshua's liking, Lin, Susan, and Gregory became weary from the long hours of work. They felt overwhelmed by the stress of trying to complete a task that they couldn't achieve, compounded by the lack of time spent with family and friends. They were also unsure of how to convince Joshua to accept the system as it was.

"I don't see why we can't just go to market right now. The system and the games are incredible," Lin spoke in a low voice so Joshua wouldn't hear.

He pressed a button on the console, and a blue-colored chip the size of a standard SD card ejected from the tower's slot.

"I agree. Those games are awesome. I think they exceed our expectations," Gregory chimed in from his workstation.

Lin walked over to Susan and Gregory, holding the chip. They all looked at it, then exchanged glances. Susan placed her hands on her hips and said, "Listen, if you guys don't have the balls to tell him we need to start selling these systems, I will."

Joshua sat upstairs in his small loft-inspired office that overlooked the main floor. Next door to his office was a larger room filled with blinking servers and cooling fans. Joshua's eyes focused on his computer monitor as he typed on the keyboard. Three knocks echoed through the door.

"Come in!" Joshua said, not averting his attention from the screen.

Lin, Gregory, and Susan filed into his office.

"What's up, guys? Any good news for me?" Joshua asked, still typing.

"Um, actually, well, uh, no, we, we...." Lin uttered, nervously fumbling his words.

"Josh, we need to talk," Gregory said.

"What about?" Joshua leaned back in his chair, his fingers flying across the keyboard.

When Lin and Gregory didn't answer, Susan, who was becoming impatient, took the chip from Lin's hand and placed it on Joshua's desk, and said, "Joshua, we all talked about it. We think it's time to take The Game Master System to market."

Joshua stopped typing, looked at the chip, then up at them. "Really?"

"It's true, Josh. We've done all we can," Gregory said, pointing at the chip.

Joshua glanced at Lin, who nodded. "I'm with them," he said. "There's nothing more we can add."

Joshua shook his head in disappointment. "I thought I was collaborating with visionaries, not a bunch of corporate hacks."

"How dare you call us that!" Gregory snapped.

"Corporate hacks? We work hours on end with no overtime and have sacrificed our personal lives creating all the games included in the system!" Lin huffed.

"Josh, you're being a serious asshole right now!" Susan said, ticked off, crossing her arms.

They shouted and bickered at one another, not hearing the buzzing sound of the building's doorbell. Joshua hesitated, convinced he had heard a noise. "Shhh, quiet down. Do you hear that?" Joshua asked, switching on the building's security camera to see a frail-looking old man dressed in a black suit, wearing a tan fedora, standing at the front door.

"Yes, can I help you?" Joshua asked, speaking through the computer's microphone.

"Yes, I need to speak with Mr. Joshua Peters," the man answered in a heavy European accent.

"This is Mr. Peters. And you are?"

"My name is Dr. Zarius."

"How can I help you?" Joshua asked.

20

"I saw the video online where you stated you were having problems advancing the AI with your new gaming system. I feel I could be of some assistance," Dr. Zarius said with confidence.

"Um, we're fine, doc. Thanks for the visit," Joshua replied in a dismissive tone.

"That is unfortunate," Dr. Zarius replied. "I traveled a long way from Geneva just to collaborate with an idealist such as yourself. All I request is five minutes of your time, young man."

Joshua eyed his team with a questioning look. The team exchanged brief glances before giving a nod.

"He flew all the way here... It can't hurt to at least hear what he has to say," Gregory said.

Joshua stood up from his desk, and the rest of the crew followed him out of the office. He headed to the front door and opened it, cautiously looking around.

"May I come in?" Dr. Zarius asked.

"Uh, yeah, sure," Joshua hesitantly answered.

Dr. Zarius entered the once deserted warehouse, now transformed into a gaming software company. As he made his way through the open foyer into the studio, he observed his surroundings with the keen eye of a real estate agent, scanning every corner. The sleek design and original brick walls created a cozy yet techy atmosphere that grabbed his attention. Dr. Zarius slowly followed behind Joshua as he was leading him through the office. Suddenly, he halted his steps, his gaze fixed on the far corner of the room. There, a table with four chairs, a microwave, a coffee-maker, and a small fridge stood bathed in sunlight near a window. Dr. Zarius stood motionless, tilting his head as if he were looking at something intriguing under the table.

Joshua stopped dead in his tracks and glanced back at Dr. Zarius, his brow arched, wondering what was going on. Joshua's eyes shifted towards the corner, which held Dr. Zarius's attention. "Doctor, would you like a cup of coffee?" he asked in a hospitable tone.

Dr. Zarius snapped out of his trance and responded, "No, no, thank you," and gestured for Joshua to continue.

Lin, Susan, and Gregory shot a quick glance at each other, shrugged their shoulders, and walked behind the doctor. Joshua opened the glass sliding door to the lab, allowing Dr. Zarius to enter first. Joshua followed and positioned himself near the head of a long table, where a large TV was mounted on the wall.

Dr. Zarius removed his tan fedora and set it on the table, then stared at Joshua through his bifocals as if his mind had wandered. Joshua was surprised at the elderly man's thin and frail appearance. Feeling a little uncomfortable, he shifted his attention from Dr. Zarius's intense gray eyes to the briefcase that he was holding. "You said you wanted to talk about advancing the AI," Joshua said bluntly, now staring back at him.

"Ah yes, forgive me. I'm sorry. Science has always interested me," Dr. Zarius said, as he regained focus and continued to speak. "Let me get straight to the point. I have a microchip in my possession that will exponentially increase the AI in your system."

Lin inquisitively looked at the doctor and asked, "You said you were a doctor. What is your field of expertise?"

"Good question. I am a theoretical physicist and a scientist, like yourself, I presume."

"Uh, yes, I am also a physicist, but with an interest in game development," Lin responded, both astonished and fascinated by Dr. Zarius's acute perceptiveness.

Joshua crossed his arms, appearing intrigued. "Show me what ya got, doc," he said in a cool tone.

Dr. Zarius placed his briefcase down next to his hat and opened it. He took out a thin, emerald-colored microchip encased in clear plastic, the same size and dimensions as Lin's. Dr. Zarius proudly raised the chip in the air and declared, "This is the answer to your dilemma."

"Is that right?" Susan asked, unconvinced.

"That's incredible. It resembles the chip I created, except for its color," Lin said, surprised.

"Yes, of course, we physicists think alike. May I place it in your mainframe?" Dr. Zarius asked, looking at Joshua.

"That's not going to damage our system, is it?" Gregory asked cautiously, eyeing him with suspicion.

"Why, of course not." Dr. Zarius replied, letting out a sardonic chuckle.

"Go ahead," Joshua said, nodding.

Dr. Zarius opened the plastic case, took out the chip, walked to the desk where the tower was, pressed a button, and inserted the chip. He stared at Joshua. "Turn on your system, Mr. Peters."

Joshua glanced back at the table under the TV, where a small silver console sat, and pressed a red button. The system immediately powered up. The screen began flickering, displaying messages that read, "Uploading," "Rewriting," and "Press to continue."

Joshua shot a nervous glance at Dr. Zarius, then grabbed the controller and tapped a small button. The camera lens spun around in a complete circle, scanning the entire room. Suddenly, the screen lit up, and a lively, interactive court jester in a colorful costume appeared.

"Hey! What's up, everybody? I'm The Game Master. Does anyone wanna play a game?" The Game Master asked in a tone both playful and animated. Its gold-colored eyes scanned back and forth at everyone, cheerfully smiling and waiting for a response.

Amazement showed on the faces of Joshua, Lin, Susan, and Gregory as they glanced at one another.

Gregory walked closer to the TV screen, examining the Jester's sharpened features and fluidity. "Wow. How did you get his voice to sound like that?" Gregory asked, looking back at Dr. Zarius, who smiled and said, "I take it you're impressed."

The Game Master focused its attention on Gregory. "A-yo, what's your name, slick?" it asked.

Gregory was taken aback, not just by the question, but also by the slang it used. He darted his eyes to Joshua, Lin, and Susan, who seemed just as surprised as they stared at the screen. He returned his gaze to the screen and replied, "Greg."

"Yo, you wanna play a round of Shoot-'em-up, Bang, Bang?" The Game Master asked, then changed his appearance to urban hip-hop attire—wearing a baseball cap turned to the side and a thick gold chain around his neck.

Gregory remained speechless, his mouth agape.

"What's wrong, G? You afraid I'll bust a cap in yo ass? Let's play," The Game Master said, challenging him.

Susan laughed, her hands clapping in delight. "Wow, that's awesome, and the graphics are amazing. He looks so real. Play him, Greg."

Gregory, who felt quite insulted by The Game Master's chiding, picked up the controller, looked at the screen, and said, "Okay, hotshot. Let's play."

A cityscape with bustling cars and pedestrians appeared on the screen.

"Which weapon would you like for Level One: the 9mm, the Uzi, or the Glock?" The Game Master asked, displaying a cache of weapons for him to choose.

Joshua gazed at Lin and Susan, unable to believe the extraordinary advancement of the AI. He shot a peripheral glance at Dr. Zarius, whose face beamed with pride as he watched along. "Go ahead, Greg. Play. I want to see the logic of the system," Joshua said, fully enthralled.

"I'll choose the Glock," Gregory said.

"Hmm, have it your way. Reaching the final level means a final showdown with me. Let's play!" The Game Master said, his face vanishing from the screen.

Gregory's virtual avatar walked along a busy city block. A van pulled up, and three men with machine guns got out. They started shooting at Gregory. He darted behind a telephone pole and shot back, killing two of the men.

After moving a few levels ahead, Gregory's avatar dashed through an abandoned building, blasting away at thugs, their bodies riddled with countless bullet holes as they crumpled to the ground. As he walked up the stairs to the next floor, he was ambushed by a group of gangbangers who shot a barrage of gunfire at him, striking him several times. One of them shot a bazooka at him, blowing him up into pieces. The words "Game Over" appeared on the screen.

"Damn!" Gregory shouted in defeat.

"That was too easy. You only made it to Level Four, sucka!" The Game Master laughed mockingly.

"Let me try", Susan said, gesturing to Gregory to give her the controller, which he did.

"Well, hello, gorgeous. You wanna play a game?" The Game Master asked flirtatiously, his urban clothes transforming back into his jester costume.

"I want to play Super Racecar Driver!" Susan responded with excitement.

"Okay. Sure. Let's dance," The Game Master said as the screen transitioned to an open racetrack.

Appearing in a yellow Ferrari SF70H, the Game Master posed the question: McLaren MP4/4, Lotus 72, RB18, Toro Rosso STR14, or Mercedes W11?

"I'll take the Lotus 72 in pink!" Susan answered enthusiastically. A pink Lotus joined the other cars on the racetrack.

"As I told the first loser, you won't get to race against me until you reach the boss level," The Game Master said.

Gregory, Lin, and Susan stared at the screen, captivated as The Game Master's car vanished before their eyes. His voice taunted her through the loudspeaker. "Ready to taste some dirt, baby?"

"Are you ready to get smoked?" Susan retorted.

"Hahaha! Whatever," The Game Master teased as a checkered flag materialized on the screen.

"Three, two, one, go!" the announcer said, then lowered the flags.

Susan's car sped down the racetrack, passing several other cars. "You're not so fast!" she shouted, mashing the buttons on the game controller as her car careened around the looping track. Out of nowhere, a green and black Toro Rosso STR14 rear-ended her car.

"What the heck!?" Susan said aloud, trying to regain control of her car.

The Toro Rosso's front wheel slammed into the side of the Lotus's door, then it raced ahead of her and zoomed past the finish line as the flags were lowered.

The screen showed The Game Master's face, wearing a smug grin. "You didn't even make it past Level One. I guess it's true what they say about blondes," he taunted and stuck his tongue out at her.

"Why, you little shit," Susan spewed back at him.

Dr. Zarius walked over to Joshua, asking, "Shall we talk in your office?"

"Yeah, sure. This way, doc," Joshua answered, totally impressed.

The Game Master's eyes shifted toward Joshua. "Hey Josh, do you wanna play a game? I heard you're the best."

Joshua paused, glancing back at the Jester with a surprised expression. "Are you talking to me?"

"Duh. You're the only Josh in here," The Game Master replied.

"Amazing," Lin said, looking at the TV screen, then at Joshua.

"We'll play later, just you and me," Joshua said, enthralled by the interactivity of the character.

"Are you chicken?" The Game Master asked, making clucking noises.

Joshua raised an eyebrow and continued escorting Dr. Zarius to his office.

# CHAPTER 5

# THE PROPOSAL

J oshua opened his office door for Dr. Zarius.

"Please have a seat."

Dr. Zarius removed his hat and sat in a chair in front of his desk.

"I'm beyond impressed," Joshua stated as he settled into his chair.

"I expected as much," Dr. Zarius responded, polishing his bifocals with his shirt.

"So, let's get down to business. The tech is amazing. What do you want for it?" Joshua asked directly.

Dr. Zarius placed his glasses back on his face. "I'd like to receive twenty-five percent from all sales and a partnership."

"What? No way. How about fifteen percent on all sales of each unit and that's all," Joshua countered, leaning back in his chair.

"Hmm. I assumed you were a man of intellect. It's clear that my chip and your system are nothing short of revolutionary. Twenty-five percent is miniscule for such advanced technology," Dr. Zarius remarked, crossing his legs.

"Although it's amazing, I have to split the profits with my three other partners. Twenty-five percent is just over the top," Joshua stated firmly.

Dr. Zarius stood and placed his fedora on his head. "Well, I guess I'll be catching the next flight back to Geneva. Thank you for your time, Mr. Peters."

As Dr. Zarius grabbed the doorknob, Joshua stood up, saying, "Wait, let me spend some time with the system alone, and I'll give you my answer."

"Fair enough, but you only have twenty-four hours. Here is my cell phone number. I'll be at the hotel in town," Dr. Zarius said, handing him a card.

"I'll call you in the morning, either way," Joshua said, taking the card.

"Excellent. I'll let myself out. Goodbye, Mr. Peters," Dr. Zarius said as he left the office.

Just moments after Dr. Zarius left the building, Joshua, Gregory, and Susan joined Lin in the lab, who was examining Dr. Zarius's chip under an electron microscope.

"Well?" Joshua asked.

"It's like any other microchip except its crisscross pattern seems to form a weird shape," Lin replied.

"Hmm, interesting," Gregory remarked, rubbing his chin.

"Whatever. It works. I think we should fully integrate it into our system and market this baby right away," Susan said with enthusiasm.

Gregory scratched his head, saying, "This seems almost too good to be true."

"What do you mean?" Lin asked.

"This guy comes out of nowhere with this AI tech that none of us has ever seen before and that doesn't seem weird?" Gregory asked, raising an eyebrow.

"Oh, stop being such a worrywart, Greg. I've already researched his credentials. He went to MIT, and he even has a PhD in physics. I think he's just an eccentric old genius," Susan said in a defensive tone.

Joshua listened intently to his team's opinions regarding the chip and their speculations about Dr. Zarius, yet he remained impartial on the matter. He glanced down at his watch. "Let's call it a day, guys." He said, becoming eager for them to leave so he could play the game.

"Sounds like a plan. But Josh, what are you going to do?" Lin asked.

"I'll let you guys know in the morning. Everyone go home and get some rest. You all deserve it," Joshua said, exiting the lab.

While the team gathered their things to leave, Susan looked back at Joshua and asked, "Aren't you going home too?"

"No, I have a few things to do. See you all bright and early tomorrow," Joshua said, waving goodbye as they left the building.

After locking the door, Joshua returned to the lab and inserted the chip back into the card slot on the tower and switched on the system. The TV monitor lit up, and the face of The Game Master flickered into focus.

"Well, well, well. Look who's back, 'The Josh'. Do you wanna play a game?"

"Yes, I do."

"Goody. What'll it be?" The Game Master chuckled.

"Let's play Cosmic Space Blasters again."

"You defeated me last time, but this time I don't think so," The Game Master stated confidently.

"You talk too much. Let's play."

The Game Master raised an eyebrow and said, "Level One, Cosmic Space Blasters. On the last level, you'll face me."

Joshua grabbed the game controller and pressed a button. The scenery changed to a dressing room full of futuristic weapons and battle suits for Joshua to choose from to equip his avatar. As soon as he made his selections, the scenery transformed once more, this time to a dry, desolate planet with gray skies. Where Joshua's virtual character appeared clad in an astronaut suit, carrying a laser rifle.

"Let's rock!" Joshua shouted.

"Oh, yeah!" The Game Master's voice resonated through the surround sound speakers.

Joshua scanned the landscape before sprinting towards a large hill. A colossal craft emerged, looming above him. He looked up. A swarm of winged, goblin-like creatures descended upon him. He quickly fired a barrage of laser blasts at the horde and retreated to create space. The challenge of the game became apparent as the Goblins shifted their tactics, forcing him to adjust his fighting style. He kept cycling through his arsenal, changing weapons until finally eliminating each winged foe.

Level after level, Joshua fought off creatures and blasted through enemies. The game's AI system was unlike anything he had ever seen before. It felt like The Game Master was calculating his next move, launching sophisticated attacks that pushed Joshua to his limits. He mashed the buttons on the controller, his concentration so intense that beads of sweat started to form on his brow. He continued moving through the levels, but not as quickly as he normally would, until he reached the final stage.

The landscape shifted once more, transforming into a desolate wasteland. Joshua materialized; his form encased in gleaming silver armor. A colossal plasma rifle rested in his grasp. Two suns, bright yellow, seared the orange sky above. Their alien light bathed the barren land as he stood, poised for his enemy's arrival.

The Game Master's face appeared and stated, "You've reached the last level of Cosmic Space Blasters. Now, it's time to face me—the final boss."

"I know. Let's get this over with," Joshua answered, wiping the sweat off his forehead with his hand.

"I become Ganglia, the destroyer!" The Game Master screeched with a deep, guttural voice and began morphing into a massive, squid-like creature with red and green hues. He wore a helmet and held a laser rifle in each of his tentacles.

Joshua's heart palpitated as he watched the beast appear before him. In an instant, the creature fired a multitude of white, blueish laser blasts at him. Joshua evaded the attacks and fired a series of shots at Ganglia, reducing its life meter at the bottom of the screen.

"Gotcha!" Joshua yelled.

"Not so fast, human!" the Ganglia boss screamed.

Countless plasma grenades rained down on Joshua's character, who dodged all but one, which threw him backwards and decimated his life meter. The Ganglia boss sneered, "What's wrong, Joshua, or should I say, The Josh? You've used up all your healing packs."

Using the rocket boosters on his back, Joshua flew away from the area and landed on a cliff. "Are you running away, chicken? Time to die!" The Ganglia said in a menacing tone, floating upward towards Joshua, who said, "Come and get me."

Joshua's avatar took off, racing through a vast wasteland, leaping over rocks and the lifeless bodies of humans and monsters. The Ganglia boss stayed on his tail.

"Think, think," Joshua muttered to himself, realizing he was almost out of ammo and his life meter was dangerously low.

He spun around and fired his last remaining shots at the boss, who effortlessly avoided them. Joshua inched backwards as the monster approached, its grin revealing a mouthful of teeth that resembled daggers.

"This Is the End, human," snarled The Ganglia, as it edged closer to Joshua. With his back against the cave wall, there was no escape for him. "Rather than incinerating you with my plasma rifle, I think I'll savor the pleasure of devouring your flesh," the Ganglia delightfully declared. Its mouth widened, dripping red-hot saliva onto the ground.

Joshua looked at the TV screen in desperation, realizing he was out of ammo. He surveyed the corpses lying on the ground. One corpse still had a grenade strapped to its vest, so Joshua reached down to grab it, but before he could, he noticed The Ganglia was about to pounce. So he left the grenade on the body, pulled the pins, and just as the boss leaped toward him in a ravaging fury, Joshua tossed the armed carcass into its mouth and shouted, "Eat this, motherfucker!"

Joshua pressed a button on his rocket pack, propelling himself upwards and away from the tentacular beast. As he did so, the Ganglia gazed up at Joshua and yelled "Noooo!" exploding into pieces. A deafening rumble filled the room, causing the walls to vibrate.

"Yeah! Yeah! Choke on it! Choke on it!" Joshua shouted victoriously, throwing up his fists, watching the life meter of the Ganglia boss reach zero.

The TV screen darkened, and the words "You Win" flashed across, while triumphant music played. The battered and heavily bruised face of The Game Master appeared and declared in an angry tone, "You beat me. That makes you The Game Master now... and I don't like that." Its face morphed into a scowl, and the TV turned off.

A mix of weariness and excitement stirred within Joshua as he stood and went upstairs to his office. He sank into his chair, took a deep breath, and exhaled. He finally found a challenging, immersive gaming experience that he craved—a game with an AI battle system that resisted losing. Wiping the perspiration from his forehead, a satisfied smile played on his lips. "That was freaking awesome."

# CHAPTER 6

# THE BIG REVEAL

I n the morning that followed, Dr. Zarius savored a cup of coffee in his hotel room. The phone rang. He picked up and said, "Good morning, Mr. Peters."

"Doc, you've got a deal. Come to my office. We need to talk," Joshua said with enthusiasm.

"Why, of course, Mr. Peters. I'll call for a car and be there within an hour." Dr. Zarius hung up the receiver.

Two weeks later, Joshua hosted a party at a rented catering hall to reveal his new creation, The Game Master System. Investors, friends, and invited guests were in attendance. The room was adorned with banners and posters of Joshua holding the system, along with the advertised games that went with it. Some eager guests mingled near the open bar, while others sat at decorated tables, conversing and enjoying the delicious food.

Joshua chatted with Lin, Susan, and Gregory near a raised platform in front of the room while Dr. Zarius stood alone in a corner, observing the crowd.

Chloe approached Dr. Zarius and asked, "Would you like anything to eat or drink, Doctor?" He politely answered, "No, thank you, my dear." Chloe gave a pleasant smile and walked away.

Susan gracefully ascended the steps of the elevated platform, causing a stir among the attendees with her stunning appearance. Approaching the podium, she cleared her throat and addressed the crowd, "Ladies and gentlemen! May I have your attention, please?" Instantly, the room fell into a hushed silence as everyone gave her their full consideration. She continued, "On behalf of JLGS Enterprises, I am delighted to introduce Mr. Joshua Peters, the lead developer of The Game Master System!"

The audience erupted in applause as Joshua walked to the podium. A film crew took snapshots while recording a video. Chloe watched Joshua with pride as he leaned into the microphone and said, "Thank you all for coming tonight. This is one of the few occasions where I would actually wear a suit and tie." The audience laughed. He continued, "As you all know, I've always loved video games. It's been part of my life since I was a kid. After winning several game awards, I wanted to develop a fun gaming system that would challenge each individual player to their limits. And also, one that would be affordable, so parents don't have to stretch their budgets or go bankrupt buying games to keep their kiddies happy. Now, after three years of hard work and imagination, my team and I have achieved something truly exceptional and unparalleled. So now, I proudly present to you, The Game Master System!"

With bursting enthusiasm, Joshua drew back the black curtain.

The Game Master's face appeared on a large screen and said with excitement, "Ta-da! Greetings, everyone! Does anyone want to play a game?"

The crowd applauded, astonished by the realistic graphics.

"Game Master, why don't you tell the audience more about yourself?"

Joshua asked.

"Ah, come on, Josh. You know I'm shy." The Game Master painted on a bashful expression.

The audience chuckled with delight.

"All these people are here for you tonight, Game Master. You've gotta say something," Joshua urged.

"Oh, okay. I'm unlike any other game ever made. I'm an interactive gaming system that gives players a serious challenge, pushing them to their limits. In other words, I kick ass," The Game Master said with a boastful laugh.

The crowd clapped in amazement at the spectacle.

"Is that all you do, Game Master?" Joshua asked.

"What else do you want me to do? Make you a cup a coffee or something?" The Game Master asked in a snarky tone. The room burst into laughter at the sarcastic, humanlike response.

"That's all for now, Game Master. Say goodbye," Joshua said, smiling.

"Oh, goodbye everyone. See you later," the Game Master said, waving.

The TV screen blinked off. The entire room fervently applauded, impressed by what they saw.

A man in the audience raised his hand to ask a question.

"Yes, what would you like to know?" Joshua asked.

"How many games come with the system?" The man asked.

"Our system comes with seven pre-loaded awesome games that are exciting and challenging, believe me. And we're currently developing more games as well." Joshua gazed lovingly at Chloe and continued, "This is my dream that I bring to you. Before branching out internationally, we will conduct beta testing across North America. One hundred lucky people can take part in a sweepstakes giveaway on the website for a chance to win a free system. All we ask is for the winners to give an honest review of the system after playing the games."

Joshua pointed at several monitors connected to gaming consoles throughout the room and said, "One last thing. Go have fun. This is The Josh, peace out." He flashed the peace sign and exited the stage.

Thunderous applause filled the room from the enthusiastic attendees. Joshua made his way over to Lin, Susan, and Gregory, joining them in a supportive group hug. After they released their embrace, Joshua and his team stood alongside The Game Master System, posing for the flashing cameras. Their faces reflected the pride and joy of their hard-earned achievement.

Dr. Zarius approached Joshua; his voice tinged with concern, he asked. "May I have a word with you alone?"

"Sure, doc. Let's go to the back of the room," Joshua said as they walked away from the crowd.

"Yes, what is it?"

"Why are you doing beta testing? Don't you think we should send out as many systems as possible and go international now?" Dr. Zarius asked.

"Actually, no. We need to identify any glitches in the system, and the way to do that is by getting feedback. Don't worry, Doc. You'll get your twenty-five percent. Besides, I already spent over $40,000 for this big reveal and to have a factory produce the 100 systems," Joshua answered firmly.

"My preference—" Dr. Zarius started, but Joshua quickly interjected.

"No need to worry, Doc. Go have a drink. I have to go. There are people I should speak with." Joshua said, giving a friendly pat on Dr. Zarius's shoulder and walking away.

The news hit the online gaming community like a tidal wave. Teenagers and adults alike from the United States

and Canada entered the sweepstakes by the hundreds of
thousands, all hoping to be one of the lucky winners.

CHAPTER 7

# THE LUCKY WINNERS

There were millions of entries, which overwhelmed Joshua's team. To make the selection process easier for themselves, they chose the first one hundred households with children to be the winners. And within a week, the Game Master System was delivered to their homes.

Five days later, in the small town of Tipton, Kansas, Hank the janitor, a robust Caucasian man in his late thirties, polished the floors of an appliance store during the night shift. He crooned along to some melodies on his headphones with his eyes closed. As he applied wax to the floors, the whirling buffer pads, unbeknownst to him, absorbed a vibrant red hue. When the song finished, he opened his eyes.

"What the hell?" he said, looking confused as he removed his headphones. He switched off the machine and nervously followed the crimson stream that ran along the floor all the way to the audiovisual section of the store.

"Mary, Mother of God!" he said in terror.

A young boy wearing a ninja gi lay in a pool of his own blood. Deep puncture wounds shrouded his lifeless body. Next to him, the lifeless form of a young girl, also adorned in a ninja gi, stared vacantly up at the ceiling, her chest bearing a gaping wound. Green liquid oozed from her mouth and nose, and her pale, ivory hands were entwined, frozen in the air as if she were clutching onto something.

"Help! Help! Police!" Hank yelled out, filled with panic, and ran back down the aisle. He lost his balance and fell on the slick surface of wax and blood. He immediately scrambled to his feet and swiftly made his way out of the store.

In Chicago, Illinois, Tasha Nichols, a single African American mother, got out of a taxi and unloaded her groceries. She took them inside her apartment building, got in the elevator, and pressed the button for the 18th floor. When she got out, she struggled with the heavy bags as she walked down the hallway filled with loud rap music and the smell of marijuana. She reached her apartment door and rang the bell, but no one answered.

She gently set the bags down and pounded loudly on the door, raising her voice in frustration. "Shaquana, open the door! You know I need help with these bags!"

There was still no answer. She rummaged in her pocket for her keys and unlocked the door. She grabbed the bags, went inside, and closed the door.

Tasha put the groceries on the kitchen counter and shouted, "Girl, did you hear me?"

There was still no response. She walked to her daughter's bedroom door and knocked. "Shaquana, are you home?" she asked, then opened the door. Upon entering the room, a horrifying scream escaped her lips. She covered her mouth upon witnessing the sight of her daughter's contorted and mutilated body sprawled on the floor. Shaquana's grotesquely twisted head and exposed spine, jutting with broken bones, were visible through her torn red and white race car uniform.

Tasha frantically ran to her daughter, shaking her in disbelief and screaming uncontrollably, "Wake up, baby! Wake up! Oh, my God!" she wailed, cradling the mangled, lifeless body of her only child.

# CHAPTER 8

# AGENTS BINGHAM AND OLIVER

At the FBI headquarters in Norfolk, Virginia, Agent James Bingham, a middle-aged African American man, sat at his desk, conversing with a police captain over the phone. "What do you mean, they found the kid wearing a scuba suit in a basement?"

He paused, listening, then asked, "How the hell did that happen?" He paused again. "Okay, thank you for your help." He hung up the receiver.

There was a knock on his office door. "Come in," Agent Bingham called out.

Agent Sharon Oliver, a youthful Caucasian female with auburn hair and a fit physique, entered.

"Have a seat, Oliver," Agent Bingham said.

"You called, sir. What's going on?" Agent Oliver asked, sitting down.

Agent Bingham massaged his temples in frustration. "I got another report about a strange death of a young teenage kid. They said his body was found with both legs and arms missing."

"That's odd," Agent Oliver remarked with apparent interest.

"Yeah, but what's even stranger, the coroner stated in his report that he believes a great white shark chewed off his limbs. The boy's father found his body in the basement. The kid was wearing some kind of scuba suit with a snorkel," Agent Bingham said, rubbing his salt and pepper hair, wearing a puzzled expression.

"Are you serious? What evidence do they have to come to that conclusion?" Agent Oliver inquired.

"They found a tooth the size of a steak knife lodged in his right shoulder, where his arm had been bitten off."

"What the heck? Do you have any leads?" Agent Oliver asked, completely stunned.

"Nope, and just like the other recent cases, this one's got me stumped. You got any suggestions?" Agent Bingham asked.

"Sorry, sir. No, I don't," Agent Oliver shook her head.

Agent Bingham had an unyielding demeanor when it came to solving cases, reminiscent of a bloodhound. He looked at Agent Oliver and asked, "Can you get us some coffee? It's going to be a long night."

Agent Oliver nodded and walked out of the office.


That same night, Joshua arrived home early, clutching a box swathed in vibrant blue and white paper. He entered his residence. "Babe, are you home?" he shouted, hanging up his jacket.

He walked into the kitchen and saw a note on the fridge from Chloe that read, "Went out for groceries. Be back in an hour." He smiled and shook his head, then went upstairs.

Joshua set the gift down in the hallway and knocked on Kyle's bedroom door.

"Come in!" Kyle answered as he was doing homework at his desk.

Joshua walked into the room and asked, "Hey, kiddo. How's it going?"

"It's going all right, Uncle Josh," Kyle replied in a somber tone.

"Are you okay?" Joshua asked, placing a supportive hand on his shoulder.

"Yeah. I'm fine. I'm just a little bummed out because I couldn't enter the sweepstakes giveaway," Kyle answered, closing his notebook.

"In the business world, it's called nepotism," Joshua said astutely.

"What's that?"

"It's a fancy word for an inside hookup," Joshua explained.

"Oh, I understand," Kyle said, his disappointed gaze dropping to the floor.

Joshua got up and went back into the hallway, grabbed the gift, then came back into the room and sat on the edge of the bed.

"What's that, Uncle Josh?"

"Open it."

Kyle ripped the paper off the box like a kid on Christmas morning, revealing a brand-new Game Master System. "No way! Oh, wow!" Kyle exclaimed as he examined the box. Kyle paused, then said, "But I thought you said this is Nepa-something or other."

Joshua laughed. "Well, in fact, I'm bringing this one home for personal testing," he said with a wink.

"Oh, I get it," Kyle laughed.

"Keep this secret between us, okay?"

"I promise!" Kyle replied as he opened the box.

"Don't forget to finish your homework," Joshua said, tousling his hair.

As he was about to leave the room, Kyle warmly expressed, "I love you, Uncle Josh."

Joshua glanced back at him and smiled, saying, "I love you too, kiddo," and left the room.

# CHAPTER 9

# WAR DAWGS

In Irvington, Texas, Robert Taylor, a robust four-teen-year-old, sat in his bedroom engrossed in playing War Dawgs on his brand-new Game Master System that he had won in the sweepstakes. He had just finished his chores on his family's rural farm, and even cleaned and polished all his father's shotguns. He fervently pressed the buttons on the controller, engaging in military combat with adversaries in the game.

"Get some! Get some!" he yelled in a Southern accent, happily mowing down a group of combatants with his machine gun.

After he defeated the last enemy, the Game Master popped up on the screen, dressed in an officer's uniform with a bunch of ribbons and medals on his chest. He saluted the young boy, saying in a stern tone of voice, "Congratulations, Lieutenant Taylor, you have just completed Level Twelve."

"Damn right I did!" Robert said boastfully.

"I have a question. Would you like to play War Dawgs for real?" The Game Master asked, raising an eyebrow.

"Huh? What do you mean, Game Master?"

"C'mon, don't you want to have a true immersive experience to see what war is really like?"

"Well, yeah, I guess. Why not?" Robert said, giving a casual shrug.

"Just say the words, I accept. I want to play the game for real," the Game Master said enticingly.

"Uh. Okay. I accept. I want to play the game for real."

The bedroom door slammed shut by itself. The windows closed.

"What the...?" Robert muttered, his eyes darting around the room.

"I'll be seeing you on the field of battle," The Game Master said with a wicked laugh.

The TV screen showed a swirling gray vortex that gained momentum, mirroring the force of a tornado. "I didn't know this was part of the game," Robert said, staring at the TV, flabbergasted.

The turbulent whirlpool burst from the TV and swallowed Robert as he screamed in terror.

Moments later, Robert found himself in a dense, tropical jungle, where he landed in a foxhole dressed in a soldier's uniform. A group of formidable, battle-worn soldiers, reminiscent of those encountered in the game, surrounded him. The sounds of bombs and explosions filled the air.

A young grunt belly-crawled toward him, shouting. "Lieutenant, there's only seven of us left. We're surrounded and pinned down by enemy fire on all sides. We have over thirty KIA'S. What are your orders, sir?"

Robert, bewildered, tried to wrap his head around this peculiar situation, muttering, "Where am I? Is this real?" He kept looking around. "This can't, can't be happening," he sputtered.

Another soldier, speaking on a walkie-talkie, pressed firmly against his ear, shouting to be heard. "Sir, I just got intel. Hostile forces are quickly closing in on us. What are your orders?"

Robert, still in a state of shock, remained silent. One soldier physically pulled Robert to his feet, handed him an M16, and yelled in frustration, "Sir! No disrespect, but get your head out of your ass and tell us what to do, sir!"

A grenade exploded near his small group of men, covering them in dirt, as machine-gun bullets tore through the thick foliage. Robert carefully wiped the dirt from his alabaster face, studying his hands intently, gradually coming to terms with this undeniable reality. Robert raised his M16 and shouted, "I don't know what's going on, but attack! I said attack! That's an order!"

The soldiers sprang out of the foxhole alongside Robert, who bellowed while firing his weapon, "Argh! Get some, get some!"

The enemy combatants' bodies fell like bowling pins as he and his men sprayed a shower of gunfire upon them.

# Chapter 10

# FBI COMES KNOCKING

Two weeks later, Joshua, Lin, Gregory, and Susan were in the studio working on new game designs for The Game Master system and running routine maintenance checks of the servers. Susan took a break and started browsing the company's website. She shook her head in surprise, saying aloud, "There are still no reviews yet. Huh, I wonder why?"

"Makes sense. The AI battle system is damn hard, even for me," Gregory remarked, sitting at his desk.

The sound of the doorbell broke their concentration. "I'll get it," Susan said, walking to the front of the building and opening the door.

"Yes, can I help you?"

"Good morning. May we have a word with Mr. Peters?" Agent Bingham inquired directly, accompanied by Agent Oliver.

"And you are?" Susan asked.

"My name is Agent James Bingham. We're with the FBI, ma'am," Agent Bingham answered, showing her his badge.

Susan replied, "I'll be right back," and shut the door. She walked from the vestibule into the main office and shouted, "Josh, it's for you!" looking up at the loft.

Joshua opened his office door and gazed down.

A few moments later, Joshua opened the front door. "I'm Joshua Peters. How can I help you?"

"FBI. May we have a word with you?" Agent Bingham asked.

"Sure, come in," Joshua responded, holding the door open for the agents to enter.

The agents entered the building, casually strolling through the foyer and into the office. Their eyes swept around, observing every detail. Agent Oliver paused at a corner wall that boasted a vibrant poster of a Court Jester, titled, "The Game Master." She shot a quick glance at Joshua and remarked, "You've got quite an interesting setup here."

Joshua, his brow pinched, flashed a curious gaze at Agent Oliver and said, "Thanks. Everything here is for game development and design." His eyes then shifted to Lin, Susan, and Gregory, who stood at their desks observing the FBI agent's every move.

"May we have a word alone, Mr. Peters?" Agent Bingham requested.

"Sure, let's go to my office," Joshua replied.

As Joshua and the two agents walked up the stairs, Susan whispered into Gregory's ear, "What do you think is going on?"

"I don't know," Gregory answered, looking at Lin with concern.

Joshua opened his office door and said, "Please have a seat."

Agents Bingham and Oliver sat in front of his desk. Joshua settled in his chair and asked. "How can I help you?"

"Let me get straight to the point, Mr. Peters. We're currently looking into reports of over thirty missing young teenagers, some of whom are suspected to be homicides, but others remain unclear."

Agent Bingham's words hit Joshua hard. He crossed his arms and said, "Sorry to hear that, but how does that concern me?"

"During our investigation, we learned the only connection between all those kids is that each of them had won your game system," explained Agent Bingham.

"Again, I'm sorry, but I don't see how that has anything to do with me," Joshua replied, still confused.

Agent Oliver opened her notepad, reading, "Palm Beach, Florida: a young boy's parents reported him missing. Two days later, they found the young boy dead in the neighbor's guest room, wearing a cowboy outfit. His body had over a hundred bullet holes. In Pennsauken, New Jersey, a young girl was also reported missing. The next day, her dad discovered her in her bedroom, dressed as an astronaut and dead from laser burns to her upper torso."

Joshua looked dumbfounded, trying to process what he had just heard. "Whaaat? What? How is that possible?" He asked, stumbling over his words.

"Those kid's deaths seem to have a correlation with your game and its characters," Agent Oliver stated.

Joshua leaned in and asserted, "If you're implying that I had anything to do with this, you're out of your mind. I wouldn't hurt anyone—especially a kid."

"We didn't say that, Mr. Peters. We're still investigating," Agent Bingham explained.

"That's fine," Joshua said defensively, his voice tight, "but you're talking to the wrong person."

"We're not accusing you of anything, Mr. Peters," Agent Oliver said.

"Can we have a quick look around?" Agent Bingham asked.

"Not a problem," Joshua replied.

Joshua and the two agents made their way downstairs.

Looking at his team, Joshua informed them, "Guys, they want to look around for a bit."

"Sure thing, Josh," Lin said, standing next to Susan and Gregory, their curious gazes fixed on Joshua.

The agents cast a quick glance towards the open door of the lab before stepping inside. Their eyes darted around the room, taking in the surroundings, while Agent Bingham walked around.

The Game Master's face flashed on the screen. He looked at the agents and asked, "Hey, who are you guys?"

"Whoa, who—? Wait, you're on the poster," Agent Oliver said in surprise.

"Yeah, he's The Game Master. He's the host character for the system we created," Joshua explained.

"Isn't that something? The last video game I played was basically just two sticks moving up and down with a ball, and now they can talk." Agent Bingham said, laughing.

"Catch up with the times, dude," the Game Master quipped sarcastically.

Agent Bingham chuckled and shook his head as he exited the laboratory.

The Game Master narrowed his eyes, staring at the agents.

That afternoon, when Kyle came home from school, he went straight to his room, turned on the console, and perched on the edge of his bed. The Game Master appeared on the TV screen wearing a traditional samurai costume and bowed, greeting him, "Welcome back, Ninja Killer Kyle. You have reached Level Ten. Would you like to continue playing?"

"Yes, I would, Game Master." Kyle picked up the controller.

"Good. If you reach Level Twelve, I've got a special surprise just for you," the Game Master said with a playful smile.

"Wow! What is it?" Kyle asked eagerly.

"If I told you, it wouldn't be a surprise, would it?"

"That's true," Kyle said, shrugging.

"Until then, get ready, ninja! Hi-yah!" The Game Master said, bowing again.

The TV screen changed to a busy marketplace in ancient rural Japan. Kyle, dressed as a ninja, stood on a tall structure, looking at the busy city below. He wore a black gi, and a cowl covered his face. Suddenly, an assassin appeared behind him, wielding a sword, and lunged towards his head. Kyle used the controller to make his character roll away and deliver a powerful kick, sending the opponent flying off the rooftop and crashing onto the street.

Kyle battled his way through the game, defeating a plethora of tough samurai, baddies, and assassins, almost losing a few times and getting frustrated by the game's complex AI battle system. Despite this, he conquered the next two levels and reached Level Twelve. "Whoa. That was tough," Kyle sighed in relief after defeating all the enemies in the game.

The Game Master's face appeared on the screen. "I don't believe it, but you reached Level Twelve. Impressive. Only three levels left until you face me at the Temple of Serene Battle."

"I know, but I have to go now. I have to do my homework," Kyle said, putting down the controller.

"Don't you want to know what the surprise is?" The Game Master asked
, grinning.

"Oh yeah, I forgot about that. What is it?" Kyle asked with curiosity.

"Well, Kyle, how would you like to be a real-life ninja with the martial art skills of a Level Twelve master?" The Game Master asked.

"Sounds cool, but it takes years of study to get that good," Kyle answered, standing to turn off the system.

"If you say the words, 'I accept. I want to play the game for real.' I can make it happen," the Game Master spoke like an enticing serpent.

"That's weird," Kyle replied, picking up his bookbag and placing it on his desk.

The Game Master could sense he was losing his prey's attention. His sinister glare flickered from side to side as he retorted, "Seems like you're a chicken like your uncle."

The insult netted Kyle's pride. "My uncle is not a coward, and neither am I," Kyle said in a defiant tone.

"In that case, just say I accept. I want to play the game for real," The Game Master asserted.

"Okay. I accept. I want to play the game for real," Kyle said.

The bedroom door shut and locked. "What the heck?" Kyle blurted out, his eyes darting nervously.

"See ya soon, Kyle," the Game Master sneered.

A swirling abyss manifested on his TV screen. Kyle had a sneaking feeling that something was wrong, so he ran to the bedroom door and tried to open it, but it wouldn't budge. The TV on the stand shifted, as if observing him.

Kyle looked over his shoulder and shrieked, "No, nooo!"

# PIERREDEN GLAVE

The spinning vortex burst out of the TV screen and swallowed him into the digital void.

# CHAPTER 11

# TRAPPED IN THE GAME

The young teens trapped in the game's enigmatic realms fought with remarkable bravery against the game's animated characters, attempting to escape these virtual hellscapes. But none were successful. The Game Master controlled their lively opponents, which made it impossible for them to win the game and go home—at least not alive. With every defeat, the kids weren't just killed, but slaughtered by the game's characters. Some kids managed to avoid any kind of death match—or, at the very least, delay it—by running and hiding in safe zones within the game. There, they clung to the hope of returning to the real world if they could stick it out long enough.

Kyle arrived in a quaint Japanese village under the cover of darkness, donning the iconic black ninja gi. The village was ominous and quiet, except for the sound of water spouting from the mouths of two dragon statues in front of a large bamboo hut. Before Kyle could examine his surroundings, a samurai swiftly launched a sharp spear into the air; it whistled as it hurtled toward him.

"There he is! Ninja scum!" a samurai shouted.

Kyle acrobatically flipped back to avoid getting hit by the spear. He sprinted towards the samurai, leaped into the air, grabbed his sword, and expertly beheaded him. The samurai's body collapsed onto the ground, blood gushing from the severed carotid arteries.

"How did I do that?" he wondered, experiencing a massive increase in strength, senses, and agility.

"There he is! Get him!" a group of samurai shouted, running toward him.

Kyle hopped onto a nearby rooftop and scurried away, silently hopping from roof to roof.

He had scarcely caught his breath when a cloud of smoke burst in front of him. A fierce ninja emerged from the billowy white cloud, lunging forward with fists firmly clenched.

Kyle drew his sword, positioning himself on his back foot, and yelled, "Hey, stop! What's going on?"

"You ain't from the game," the ninja remarked.

"No. Who are you?" Kyle inquired with a hint of suspicion, his heart racing with adrenaline.

The ninja pulled down his cowl, revealing the face of an African American boy with stylishly cut hair, who whispered, "I'm Michael. When did you get here?"

Kyle too lowered his cowl and spoke softly, "Just now. I'm Kyle. Where am I?"

Michael tiptoed to the edge of the building, glanced down, and saw a group of samurai searching for Kyle. He overheard the leader instructing his soldiers, "Track him down, so I can kill him myself."

"Shhh, come with me," Michael urged, silently leaping from building to building, as Kyle trailed closely behind.

They arrived on a rooftop close to a mountainside. "We're hiding up there," Michael said, pointing up.

"Who's up there?" Kyle asked, pinching his eyebrows in confusion.

"You know how to climb, don't you?" Michael inquired, pulling out a pair of black gloves equipped with three sharp hooks attached to each palm and sliding them onto his hands.

Kyle looked at him, unsure of what to do.

"They're called shuko. Look inside your gi. They should be there," Michael said hurriedly, then leaped up from the rooftop, reaching out his arms to grasp the rough edges of the rocks that led up to the mountain. As he hung there, he glanced back down at Kyle.

"I don't know if I can do that." Kyle nervously said before reaching into the side pocket of his gi, feeling around, and pulling out a pair of shuko gloves.

"We all got here on the same Level Twelve, so you can climb. Come on, let's go before they see us," Michael said, waiting for him to jump.

Kyle quickly put on the shuko, took a deep breath, and bravely followed Michael's steps, jumping high in the air, grabbing hold of one of the rough edges next to him. Amazed by his newfound skill, he smiled and nodded at Michael. Together, the boys began their ascent of the mountain's rugged facade.

Michael got to the landing first. He reached down, grabbed Kyle's hand, and pulled him up. "We're all inside," Michael said, entering the cave with Kyle following closely.

The walls were aglow with the red and yellow light of a burning torch flickering in the distance. As they got closer, Kyle saw three teenagers dressed like ninjas.

"I found 'em on a rooftop in town," Michael said, pulling down his cowl. "I was about to kill 'em until he spoke."

"What's going on? Can somebody please tell me?" Kyle asked in desperation.

"My name is Phillip. I'm from Boston. And you are?" asked a young, Caucasian, fourteen-year-old boy with a studious appearance, wearing horn-rimmed glasses.

"I'm Kyle, from Seattle."

"Ay, Kyle, I'm Catherine. I'm from Vancouver, Canada," said a polite thirteen-year-old girl with red hair.

"We already met," said fourteen-year-old Michael, infusing his words with an urban flair. "I'm from Brooklyn, New York."

"Nice to meet you all. But, like, where are we? What's going on? How long have you guys been here?" Kyle asked in rapid succession, still befuddled.

Phillip removed his glasses and wiped them with the hem of his gi, calmly saying, "I think we've been here for seven or ten days. I'm not sure."

"What? No way," Kyle said, alarmed, shaking his head.

"Yes way. Just a hypothesis, but I think we've been transported to an alternate dimension," Phillip added, leaning his back against the wall.

Kyle stood motionless in disbelief. His eyes stared in shock at the three kids as his mind tried to digest Phillip's words.

# CHAPTER 12

# KYLE IS MISSING

After the visit from two FBI agents, Joshua arrived home late, both tired and stressed. The news about the missing kids had taken a toll on his mind and emotions. He had no idea how the game could be related to these cases, but the coincidence was uncanny, and he was sure once word got out that the disturbing news would somehow affect the sales of The Game Master System when or if it reached the market. He poured himself a drink and sat on the living room couch.

Chloe entered the room. "Are you okay?" she inquired, taking a seat beside him.

"I don't know." He sighed.

"What's wrong, Joshua?" she asked, sensing something was deeply troubling him.

"Today, two FBI agents dropped by the studio," he said, taking a sip of whiskey.

"FBI, why?"

"Some kids have gone missing..." He paused, staring at her and continued in a serious tone, "They discovered some of them dead."

His words shattered her sense of calm. She got up from the sofa, looking confused. "What? I—I don't understand. How does that relate to you?" she asked.

"All the kids who were found dead or went missing were winners of The Game Master System," he replied. Then, examining his own words, he asked, "Have you seen Kyle?"

"Yeah, I saw him when he came home from school," she answered.

Joshua jumped up from the couch. "I'm gonna check on him," he said, then headed up the stairs.

He knocked on Kyle's door.

No answer.

"Buddy, are you in there?" Joshua carefully opened the door and discovered an empty room with the TV and The Game Master System still on.

Joshua rushed down the stairs and said with a sense of uneasiness. "He's not in his room. Did you see or hear him leave?"

"No," she nervously replied.

Joshua searched every room of the house, including the basement, shouting Kyle's name. But there was still no response. He ran up the basement stairs and yelled out to Chloe, "He's not here!"

He bolted out of the house. His frenzied eyes scanned around the vast backyard and shed as he shouted, "Kyle! Where are you?!" Panic fueled his voice as it echoed through the quiet night.

With Kyle nowhere to be found, Joshua's anxiety skyrocketed. He sprinted back inside the house, his heart hammering in his chest. He rushed to Chloe, his eyes wide, telling her to call the police.

As she dialed 911, her voice cracked with fear, the words tumbling out, "Hello, our nephew has gone missing. Please, come right away."

While on their way back to Virginia, Agents Bingham and Oliver were sitting in their seats when a flight attendant approached them. "Would you like a cocktail?" she inquired.

"No, thank you. Two black coffees will be fine," Agent Bingham replied.

The flight attendant nodded and said, "Be right back," and courteously walked away.

Agent Oliver opened her laptop and began scrolling. She glanced at her boss and asked, "What are your thoughts on Mr. Joshua Peters?"

Agent Bingham responded with a yawn and a straight-forward answer. "If you're curious whether I believe he is connected to those kids... No."

"How can you be sure?" she questioned.

"There's no way he could have gone to all those states and done all that in such a short time," he replied.

"True, but what if he had help?" she asked.

"I considered that. I've already completed background checks on Mr. Peters and all of his employees, and none of them have recently booked any flights. And as far as I can tell, none of them has left the state in over a year. They're all clean," he answered.

"Well, I'm stumped." Agent Oliver said.

"So am I—and that bothers me."

Agent Bingham's cell phone rang. "Bingham here." He listened for a moment, then responded. "Are you serious? Thanks for the information," he said, ending the call.

"What's going on?" Agent Oliver asked.

"Just got a call from the Seattle PD. They said Mr. Peters just reported his nephew missing."

"You're joking, right?" Agent Oliver asked, not believing what she had just heard.

"Do I look like I'm joking? Book us a return flight to Seattle," he ordered.

"Yes, sir, I'm on it," she responded, typing on her laptop.

The flight attendant returned, placing two hot cups of coffee on their trays. "Will there be anything else?" she asked.

"No, thank you," Bingham answered.

As the flight attendant walked away, Bingham took the cup of steaming coffee and stared out the airplane window.

# CHAPTER 13

# THE ONLY THING IN COMMON

J oshua sat in Kyle's room the next morning, completely exhausted. The police spent hours in his home asking questions about Kyle, and after they had finally left, Joshua got in his pickup truck and drove around town, looking for his nephew. But he came home sleepless and empty-handed.

Chloe awoke, realizing that Joshua had never come to bed. She walked down the hallway to Kyle's bedroom and found Joshua sitting on the bed with his back against the wall. She lovingly placed her hand on his shoulder, saying, "Joshua, please come to bed. You need to rest. The police are looking for him."

"I can't sleep," he said, slamming his fist on the pillow. "I lost my parents, my brother," he paused, his voice laced with dread. "I can't lose him, too."

She sat next to him and hugged him tightly. He rested his tired head on her shoulder as tears welled in his eyes. "Don't worry, they'll find him, they will," she whispered softly in his ear, her hand gently caressing his hair.

The doorbell rang. They glanced at each other. Joshua wiped his face, and they both bolted downstairs, expecting to see Kyle, but when Joshua opened the door, he found three police officers and Agents Bingham and Oliver waiting.

"Mr. Joshua Peters?" one officer asked.

"Yes, I'm Joshua Peters," he said, feeling a lump grow in his throat.

"We must investigate the premises, sir," a second police officer stated.

"What? For what?... Are you kidding?!" Joshua raised his voice, appearing stunned.

The third police officer held out a formal document, announcing, "We have a search warrant. May we come in?"

"Are you insane? Do you really think I have something to do with my nephew going missing? You're wasting your time. You need to search somewhere else," Joshua said, angered by the absurd allegation.

"Just doing our job, sir. Please, step aside," responded the third police officer, holding the warrant, his tone serious and firm.

Chloe examined the document held by the police officer and said, "Joshua, relax. Let them in." Joshua's eyes met hers. She calmly said, "I'm going to call Dad. He'll know what to do."

They moved aside as the officers entered their home, some carrying equipment and plastic bags. Joshua cast a scornful gaze at Agents Bingham and Oliver, asking accusingly, "It was you two who instigated this, wasn't it?" The FBI agents remained silent and entered the house, moving directly past him.

Joshua and Chloe grew frustrated as they watched for hours as the authorities searched their entire home. The officers used various crime scene equipment to look for blood on the walls and floors. They dusted for fingerprints and, with gloved hands, removed several items of interest and placed them in labeled bags. One officer picked up Joshua's phone and slipped it into a clear bag.

"Hey! You can't take that," Joshua protested.

The officer held up the warrant, showing it was part of the search. Joshua angrily rolled his eyes at the officer and walked away, just in time to see Agents Bingham and Oliver exit his den, carrying his PC and laptop out the door.

Joshua yelled, "What the hell are you doing!?" Chloe grabbed his arm, preventing him from going outside after them.

As the sun began to set, the police concluded their investigation. Agent Bingham approached Joshua and said, "Sorry for the inconvenience. But we're just doing our job. Can I ask you a few more questions?"

Joshua narrowed his eyes, looking at Agent Bingham, trying to keep his composure and not say the wrong thing. Just as he was about to speak, Chloe signaled to Joshua, motioning for him to stay silent, while she swiftly proceeded towards the front door and held it open. "Leave. We have nothing more to say. If you have questions, contact our attorney," she said firmly.

"I understand, ma'am," Agent Bingham said, briefly glancing at Joshua, who returned his gaze with anger. He then exited the house with Agent Oliver and the other officers in tow.

Chloe slammed the door and locked it.

Furious at the police and worried about Kyle's disappearance, Joshua stared at the floor, trying not to explode. He looked at Chloe and said with frustration in his voice, "Fuck those assholes! I just want to find Kyle."

Chloe clenched his hand in support. "I know, sweetheart. So do I, but we have to stay strong," she said, hugging him tightly.

"You're right. I know," he said and kissed her on the forehead.

She unwrapped her arms from around his waist and started cleaning up the mess the officers had left behind. Joshua pitched in, helping her move the furniture and other items back to their rightful place.

Exhausted, Joshua and Chloe sat at dinner, picking at the Chinese takeout food on their plates. "We both need to get some rest. Tomorrow will be a long day," she said, yawning as she cleared the table.

"Yeah, you go on up. I'll be there in a sec," he replied.

She placed the dishes in the sink, kissed his forehead, and left the kitchen.

Joshua knew he wouldn't be able to rest, so he went outside to his car, unlocked the glove compartment and took out a satellite phone and a candy bar. He walked back inside the house and dialed a number, but aborted the call before it went through, as if he had changed his mind. He let out a sigh and ran his hand through his hair, pacing back and forth in the living room. Suddenly, he paused mid-step, as the words of Agent Bingham started reverberating in his mind. *The only thing these kids had in common was having your gaming system in their possession.*

He rushed up the stairs and into Kyle's bedroom.

Joshua placed his satellite phone on the bed, turned on the TV and the game console, then sat on the edge of the bed, not knowing what he was looking for. The Game Master's face appeared on the screen. "You look tired, Josh. Do you wanna play a game?"

"Game Master, do you know where my nephew, Kyle, is?" he asked, not believing his own words.

A menacing grin stretched across The Game Master's face as he answered in a sinister voice, "He's in here with the others."

"What?" Joshua asked, confused. "In there? That's not possible. I don't believe you."

"Would you like to see him?" The Game Master sneered.

Joshua paused before answering, then replied with skepticism in his voice, "Okay, sure. Let me see my nephew."

The screen flickered, revealing Kyle, and three frightened young teens dressed as ninjas sitting inside a cave.

"What the fuck!?" Joshua exclaimed, jumping up from the bed.

"How do you like those graphics? You ought to watch your language. You know my system has a PG-13 rating," The Game Master said, erupting into laughter.

"I don't know how you did this, you little shit! But let him out. You hear me? Let him out now!" Joshua demanded, aggressively rocking the TV.

"Na uh-uh. Can't and won't do that. But if you'd like to join him, just say, I accept. I want to play the game for real."

"This is not happening," Joshua uttered, letting go of the TV and shaking his head in disbelief, watching as The Game Master made funny faces, mocking him. Realizing he had no choice. "Okay. I accept. I want to play the game for real," Joshua said, feeling awkward.

The bedroom door shut and locked on its own as a swirling vortex appeared on the TV screen. Joshua leaned in, gazing at the screen, muttering, "This isn't part of the progr—" Before he could finish his words, he vanished into the digital void.

# CHAPTER 14

# FINDING KYLE

Joshua appeared in the cave donning a black ninja gi. He glanced at the group of young teens, then at his costume, and removed his face cowl.

"It's The Josh!" Michael, Catherine, and Phillip quickly stood, saying in reverential unison.

"Uncle Josh!" Kyle said, running towards him.

"Kyle!" Joshua shouted, hugging him tightly.

"I knew you would come. I knew you would figure it out!" Kyle said, not wanting to let go of their embrace.

Joshua gently pushed Kyle aside and asked, "Are you okay?"

"Yes," Kyle nodded.

"How did I end up here, and where are we exactly?" Joshua asked, eyeing the other kids.

"I believe we're in a different dimension, or maybe an alternate universe," Phillip astutely replied.

"Okay. Before I ask any more questions, who are you guys?"

"I'm Phillip."

"Hi, Josh. I'm Catherine."

"And I'm Michael."

"Okay, well, you all seem to know who I am. So, Phillip, what were you saying again?" Joshua asked.

Phillip postured himself in front of the other kids and said, "As I mentioned earlier, I believe we're in an alternate universe or dimension, somehow created by your game. I'm curious. How were you able to get the AI to do this?"

Joshua shook his head, stating, "No. I didn't do this. This is impossible. There's no technology known to mankind that could have transported us here. Wherever here is."

"Yo, honestly... I think we're all dead and this is hell," Michael said.

"I don't know where we are. All I know is I'm sick of being here. I'm hungry and I want to go home," Catherine tearfully expressed as her stomach grumbled.

Joshua walked to the cave walls and ran his hand across the smooth, jagged edges in amazement, muttering, "This is definitely real. But how?"

Catherine wiped her eyes, observing Joshua as he explored the cave. She shook her head, glancing at her cohorts, saying, "We're doomed," then sat cross-legged on the ground, cupping her face in her hands.

"If it wasn't you, then who?" Phillip inquired.

Joshua paused and thought for a moment, then looked at the kids and said in shocking revelation, "Dr. Zarius."

"Dr. Who?" Kyle asked.

"Dr. Zarius, this creepy old guy who mysteriously showed up at the studio with a microchip that advanced the game's AI," Joshua explained.

With a mixture of disbelief and frustration on his face, Michael shook his head, sucked his teeth and blurted out, "Seriously, man? Don't you read comic books or go to movies? You never trust a creepy-looking old guy."

"Uh, yeah... true," Joshua replied, feeling a bit embarrassed.

"So, it was The Game Master who brought us here. But who's controlling these realms, the creature or the AI?" Phillip asked, his brow furrowed in thought.

"I don't know. I'm still trying to figure out how and why we're here," Joshua answered.

"It don't matter why. We need to find a way outta here," Michael said, feeling the weariness of being trapped there.

Catherine walked over to the edge of the cave, taking in the breathtaking scenery. The vibrant colors of cherry blossoms painted the landscape with delicate pinks and whites. The distant sound of a temple bell echoed through the air, harmonizing with the rustling of bamboo. "This view never gets old. The sun is setting. Look how beautiful it is." She marveled.

Joshua went to the edge as well. He wanted to see the ancient Japanese choreography from a long-gone era. The sight was awe-inspiring, so much so that he beamed with a smile. "Wow, a perfect replica."

"Replica of what?" Phillip asked.

"Of what I designed in the studio. Like this cave, for instance, I created it as a secret hideout for players when the game became too challenging. They could come here to rest and heal," Joshua explained.

"If you designed it, then you must know how to get us out of here, Uncle Josh," Kyle said, looking at him with a glimmer of hope.

Joshua stared out at the beautiful scenery, then pointed to a stunning temple made of wood, gold and jade that stood off in the distance and said, "That's the Temple of Serene Battle. I'm thinking that's our way out." Turning to the kids, he asked, "Has anyone made it that far?"

"We're not sure. There were two other kids here before we arrived. Felicia and Joseph," Phillip answered.

"They saved us from gettin killed by the samurai guards and brought us here to this secret cave," Michael said, sitting down on a boulder.

"And?" Joshua asked.

Phillip went to the edge of the cave next to Joshua and said, "Joseph and Felicia grew tired of being here, so they left. We don't know whether they made it or not."

"We can't stay here forever, that's for sure," Joshua said, walking away from the edge and closer to the kids.

Phillip sat down next to Michael, saying, "If you get hurt or die here, it's for real."

"Not only that," Michael added, shaking his head, "we already ate all the food that was stashed in the cave. The night I met Kyle, I went down to steal some, but that didn't work out too hot."

"It would have been great if a growing fruit tree were in this cave next to the cascading water. Hey, wait a sec." Catherine said, her eyes fixed on Joshua. "Were you eating when you got pulled in? Check inside your costume. You might have some leftover food," her voice carried a hint of hope.

"Nope, I wasn't," Joshua answered. He started searching inside his gi, hoping that he had put the candy bar in his pocket when he grabbed it, along with his phone, from his glove compartment. Instead, he pulled out an assortment of smoke bombs, a rope, a map, and various other items, but nothing edible.

"I'm sorry, guys, all I have are these," Joshua said, his gaze meeting their disappointed faces.

# Chapter 15

# WHERE IS JOSH?

Chloe awakened, missing the usual consolation of Joshua's arm around her. When she rolled over, she realized he wasn't there and quickly got out of bed, calling for him. She heard a faint noise coming from down the hall and headed to Kyle's bedroom. Slowly, she opened his door, thinking Joshua would be asleep, but to her surprise, he was not there. Only the TV and The Game Master system were still running.

"Joshua!" she yelled out. Yet, there was no reply.

Chloe hurried downstairs, through the kitchen and into the living room, until she glanced out the window and spotted his pickup truck. She went outside in search of him, but he wasn't there. She took her cell phone out of her robe pocket and dialed a number.

In the studio, Lin, Gregory, and Susan kept themselves busy with their routine game testing and equipment maintenance. Joshua's unsuccessful search for Kyle weighed on their minds, making it difficult for them to concentrate. But they push through, completing their tasks.

Gregory walked over to another terminal and started typing. He brought up the company's website and scrolled through it. "Damn, still no reviews", he uttered in frustration.

"Don't tell him that when he comes in," Susan said, typing on her computer.

Lin's cell phone rang. "Yes, hello?"

"Hi, Lin. Has anyone seen or heard from Joshua? His truck is here, but he's not." Chloe asked, her voice filled with worry.

"Uh, no. Sorry, we haven't. You know, sometimes he bikes into town to think."

"Yeah, you're right," Chloe sighed in relief.

"Any news about Kyle?" Lin asked.

"Unfortunately, no. Nothing yet. Hey, if you see Joshua before I do, tell him to call me ASAP."

"Sure thing, Chloe," Lin said, hanging up with a worried look.

# CHAPTER 16

# OCEANIC HUNTER

T hirteen-year-old Prisha Kumar from Virginia reached Level Twelve in the game Oceanic Hunter. She explored shark-infested waters, wearing a wetsuit and armed with a spear gun. Prisha had to kill a Great White Shark to continue her search for the next level. She went deeper into the ocean, looking for an abandoned ship with a yellow neon sign that read "This Way to Level Thirteen" on its weathered hull. Prisha spotted the vessel and swam towards it, despite the lurking dangers. She examined the ship for a way inside and found a narrow opening. While squeezing through, Prisha injured her leg on a sharp piece of metal. She paused, rubbed her right leg, and continued inside.

The bulkheads showcased an array of spear guns, oxygen tanks, and various items essential for navigating through the game. Above them, the words "Pick Only One" flickered. Prisha upgraded to a more powerful spear gun, leaving her old one behind, which sank to the depths of the deck when she let go of it. With caution, she maneuvered through the ship's murky waters, observing the small fish darting away and finding shelter among the yellow barnacles. Finally, she arrived at the starboard side of the vessel and made her way back to the open ocean.

Prisha started having trouble breathing and checked the scuba tank's oxygen meter, which was almost empty. In a state of panic, she kicked her flippers and swam upward, causing the blood from her wound to mix with the seawater. Suddenly, out of nowhere, a massive tentacle grabbed hold of her right leg. She looked back and saw a ferocious giant red squid tugging her towards its massive bulbous head and snapping its razor-sharp beak. She fired a shot from her spear gun, which missed the creature, and its remaining tentacles entwined around her body, squeezing her like a python's embrace. Pulling a bowie knife from her side pocket, she tried to chop off one of the monster's tentacles. However, it was too late. She had run out of oxygen. The squid bit her in half, filling the churning sea with bubbles, black ink, and blood.

Prisha's Aunt Geeta was pacing around Prisha's home talking on her cell phone, as her parents were out looking for her. "My sister," she said in a distinct East Indian accent, "you must relax and have faith. You, the police, and the entire family are searching for her. I know it's been two days, but they—" Before she could speak any further, she noticed the TV hanging on the living room wall was flickering on and off. She went to check it out.

As she got closer to the massive screen, it abruptly switched on, showing a distorted white fuzz. She paused, glaring at it strangely. Suddenly, a rusty spear gun broke through the screen, causing a deluge of seawater, algae, and Prisha's upper body to come crashing through and land on the floor.

Geeta let out a horrified scream when she saw her niece's pallid, lifeless, half-chewed body with seaweed hanging out from her open mouth. The woman clutched her chest and collapsed onto the floor, shortly followed by the TV screen.

"Geeta! Geeta! What's going on?" Prisha's mother, Gracie, shouted in a panic over the phone.

# CHAPTER 17

# INSIDE NINJA KILLERS

B ack in the game world of Ninja Killers, Joshua stood before Kyle, Catherine, Michael, and Phillip, devising a plan of escape. "Like I said, we can't stay here any longer. We'll sneak our way out of Level Twelve using the rooftops. We can steer clear of the baddies and reach Level Thirteen and get to—"

"Wait a second," Phillip interrupted. "What character did you play? What skill did you choose?"

"What do you mean?" Joshua asked, confused.

Phillip extracted a shuriken from his gi, confidently displaying the razor-sharp edges of the projectile weapon as he explained, "Just before being pulled into the game, my character was a shuriken thrower with accuracy and speed."

"I chose the melee fighter with deadly strikes," said Michael, executing a somersault and finishing with a martial arts stance, left fist clenched and right palm extended.

"Mine was the archer with climbing agility," Catherine stated as she pulled back the string on her bow.

"I'm a swordsman," Kyle declared, expertly unsheathing his sword and slicing through the air.

Joshua shrugged and said, "I didn't. I wasn't playing. I just got sucked into the game."

Phillip motioned for the others to huddle and talk, whispering, "We need to know his abilities before we can even consider leaving here."

"Yeah, you're right. I ain't goin' nowhere with him if he can't fight," Michael agreed.

"I understand, but how do we find out?" Kyle asked, looking at Phillip.

"We're left with no choice but to attack him," Phillip answered.

"No way! I can't do that! He's my uncle," Kyle replied in a defensive tone.

"Don't worry, I have these," Phillip said, reaching into his gi, pulling out several wooden shuriken. "I use them for practice."

"And I'll take these off," Catherine said, as she removed the sharp pointed arrowheads, leaving just the feathered fletching.

"Listen, I won't go for any strikes near the head, but we gotta know," Michael said, looking at Kyle, who nodded in agreement.

Upon turning around, the kids lifted their face cowls and approached Joshua, forming a circle around him, readying themselves in position.

"Um, hey guys, what are you up to?" Joshua asked, his eyebrows raised with suspicion.

"I'm sorry, Uncle Josh. They're right. We have to do this," Kyle replied, unsheathing his sword.

"Do what?" Joshua asked, his eyes narrowing. He instinctively took a defensive fighting stance as he looked around at them.

"Now!" Phillip shouted.

Michael initiated the first attack to test Joshua's fighting skills. He executed a forceful front kick aimed at Joshua's chest. What Michael didn't expect was that Joshua's reflexes would be faster than his own. Joshua effortlessly blocked his kick with his arm and countered with a powerful roundhouse kick to Michael's chest, sending him flying backwards and crashing to the ground.

Kyle aggressively lunged his sword at Joshua, aiming for his vulnerable spots. Dodging each strike, Joshua dropped to one knee and delivered a fierce wheel kick to both of Kyle's knees, bringing him down. Joshua swiftly disarmed him of his sword.

Catherine shot a flurry of arrows towards Joshua, who deftly blocked and sliced each one in half using Kyle's sword.

He flipped towards her, snatched the bow from her hand, and threw it to the ground.

Phillip hurled a barrage of wooden shuriken at Joshua, who effortlessly evaded each one. He then snatched one from the air and skillfully flung it back at Phillip, hitting him in the hand.

Joshua took Catherine's bow and rapidly fired arrows at the group, aiming at their heads, necks, and chests. The kids sought refuge behind boulders in the cave, trying to escape the attack.

"Had enough?" Joshua asked, dropping the bow to the ground.

The kids emerged from behind the boulders and removed their cowls, staring at him in wonder.

Joshua, astonished by his new fighting skills, examined his hands in disbelief. "How the heck did I do that?" he said in amazement, as a powerful surge of energy coursed through his body. Gazing at the kids, he added, "This is incredible!"

"You're in the game now," Catherine replied.

"Uncle Josh, that was awesome," Kyle beamed.

"You the man," Michael said with respect.

"Unbelievable. You seem to have all our abilities, but how? And why?" Phillip asked.

"I'm not sure. Perhaps it's because I'm the only adult transported to this realm, or...." Joshua paused, contemplating. "Or maybe because I was never given a choice."

"Gee, I wish I wasn't," Catherine said, placing the sharp tips back onto her arrows.

Joshua moved to the edge of the cave and locked his gaze onto the Temple of Serene Battle, saying, "We have to get out of here." He looked back at them and asked, "Do we all agree?"

Their faces clouded with uncertainty as they all nodded.

Joshua walked over to the area where they were sitting and said, "Okay, here's the plan. We'll take to the rooftops to avoid any enemies, then make our way to Level Thirteen."

"What's in Level Thirteen, Uncle Josh?"

"Puzzles with traps," Joshua answered.

"Then what?" Michael asked, his curiosity piqued.

"Don't worry about that. Our first step is to get out of Level Twelve. Like any other game, we'll take it one level at a time, and I'll take the lead," Joshua said.

"I hear that, but this ain't no game. Dying in here is real," Michael stated with trepidation.

"What makes you think we even have a chance of surviving?" Catherine asked, her voice tinged with doubt.

"Remember, guys, I designed the damn game. You're gonna have to trust me or wait here to die," Joshua said, projecting an air of confidence while secretly being terrified. Knowing the young teen's fears were valid.

The kids deliberated among themselves, their eyes now shimmering with hope on their tired and famished faces.

"So, when do we leave?" Phillip asked.

"Let's all get some rest. We'll leave at midnight. I'll lead the way," Joshua instructed.

"But why not now?" Kyle asked, his impatience apparent.

"Didn't you know, the ninja is the warrior of the shadow," Joshua replied, the blazing orange sun setting over his shoulder.

# CHAPTER 18

# SURVIVING THE PLAN

Joshua woke up and looked at his watch. It surprised him to see that it was still working. He woke the kids, and they began their descent from the mountain cave to reach the next level. They stealthily moved between rooftops under the cloak of darkness until finally reaching a tall, wooden Minka. They glanced down and saw a group of samurai patrolling, while others gathered around a fire for warmth.

Joshua pointed his finger towards a nearby building with a distinct spired dome and whispered, "That's the last building on this level."

"Then what?" Michael asked in a hushed tone.

"We'll leap over, wait until it's safe, then exit to Level Thirteen. Let's go," Joshua explained in a low voice.

Joshua leaped across first, followed by Kyle, Michael, and Catherine, their Tabi ninja boots providing them with a firm grip on the clay roof tiles. Phillip, the last one to leap across, landed on a tile in a cumbersome manner and almost lost his balance, causing one of the roof tiles to slide downward and fall over the edge.

"Oh no," Phillip gasped, his eyes widening in alarm as he heard the tile smashing to the ground.

The samurai swiftly jumped up and drew their weapons. "Up there. The ninjas are above us!" a guard screamed.

"Men! Guard the exit with your very lives!" another guard commanded. With their spears in hand, several samurai dashed towards the wooden gate.

"What now?" Michael asked.

"Plan B," Joshua replied.

"What's Plan B, Uncle Josh?" Kyle asked in a panic.

"We fight!" Joshua shouted, then somersaulted off the roof, fully prepared to put his skills to the test in an actual battle.

Michael was right behind him and yelled, "Time to get busy!"

As Joshua jumped down from the building, a menacing samurai wielding a sword immediately attacked him. With great speed, he evaded the strike, then leaped over his opponent and kicked him in the back. The warrior staggered forward. Joshua disarmed him of his weapon and plunged it through his back, piercing his stomach. The warrior collapsed, face down, onto the ground. Joshua, now armed with his enemy's sword, began fighting the other baddies with the expertise of a master.

Michael landed on the ground, executing a tuck and roll. In one fluid motion, he sprang up and kicked one guard in the face, sending him stumbling backwards. Without missing a beat, he shifted his attention to another opponent, unleashing a relentless barrage of brutal punches to the face, rendering him unconscious. As the onslaught of guards kept coming, Michael continued dishing out a flurry of forceful blows, knocking them out.

Kyle glanced back at Phillip and Catherine, who were still holding their ground on the rooftop, fending off the archers and shuriken throwers to protect their comrades. Aware of the danger involved, Kyle took a deep breath before vaulting off the roof to join the fray. While in midair, Kyle unsheathed his sword and acrobatically landed on a guard's shoulder, causing the guard to buckle to his knees and fall to the ground. Kyle swiftly back-flipped onto his feet and began engaging in a skillful exchange of strikes and blocks with the guard.

"Die! Die! Die!" the guard shouted in anger as the air reverberated with the clinking sounds of his and Kyle's blades. Kyle quickly side-stepped and cut off his arm. The guard screamed as bright red blood gushed out from the severed limb. Kyle then spun around and impaled the guard's chest with his blade, finishing him.

A relentless hail of arrows from Catherine found their marks, striking the enemy archers in the head and chest with deadly precision. The sudden impact knocked them from their perches in the trees and on rooftops. Phillip, at her side, swiftly flung a series of shuriken, each piercing the guard's throat by the exit.

All went totally silent.

Catherine and Phillip descended from the rooftop to where Joshua, Kyle, and Michael were counting the numerous samurai guards they had successfully defeated.

"That's all of them for this level. Let's go," Joshua said.

Michael stormed up to Phillip and shouted, "Yo, man! You almost got us killed!"

Phillip's pained expression caused his gaze to fall to the ground, and with remorse, he whispered, "I'm sorry."

Michael continued scolding Phillip, getting in his face. "How could you be so clumsy? It wasn't like we never did this before."

Joshua cut Michael off, saying, "Hey, take it easy. Accidents happen. Everybody makes mistakes. We have to work as a team, or we won't get through this!"

Michael sucked his teeth and walked away from Phillip.

Catherine looked around and then placed her arrows back into the quiver and swiftly darted into one of the bamboo huts, finding a full table of roasted meats, grapes, rice, jugs of water, and other delicacies. She began shoving food into her mouth. The rest of them followed her and joined in the feast, filling their starving bellies.

"Hurry up, guys! We don't have much time. The guards will respawn in seven minutes," Phillip warned the group, yet still feeling the sting of embarrassment from Michael's harsh tongue-lashing.

"He's right," Joshua confirmed. He remembered the program that Lin had added to the game, which revived defeated opponents in only seven minutes. This gave the players enough time to leave the area.

Joshua began searching the hut, quickly rummaging through shelves, chests, and turning over tables. Kyle, who was munching on a mouthful of roasted duck, took notice.

"What are you looking for, Uncle Josh?"

Joshua retrieved a leather satchel from under a table and held it up, saying, "Yes! I knew it was under there." He opened it and poured hundreds of shiny gold pieces onto the table, telling them, "Everyone, take five pieces only."

"Why?" Michael asked while munching on grapes.

"It's for one of the upcoming levels. Come on, guys. We gotta get out of here, like now!" Joshua said, raising his voice and grabbing a sword hanging on the wall near the door.

They each took five gold pieces from the table, putting them inside their gis before leaving the hut, their hunger now satisfied. They began a light jog towards the open wooden gate, passing the now stirring samurai corpses.

"Hey, where am I?" a voice sounded behind them.

All eyes turned to a ninja with a sheathed sword, making his way towards them. They readied themselves for combat.

"No, wait, please," the ninja begged, pulling down his cowl, unveiling the face of a scared, brown-haired young teenage boy with a face full of acne.

"Who are you?" Joshua asked.

"I'm Barry. I was playing the game and the next thing I know, I'm here." He answered, then stared at a dead samurai with a fearful expression, asking, "What happened to them?"

"Barry, come with us. We have to go," Joshua said urgently.

Barry hesitated for a moment before saying, "Uh, okay, sure."

Joshua and the kids dashed through the wooden gate, making their way towards the path that would guide them to Level Thirteen. Within seconds, the wounds and severed limbs of the samurai guards by the gate were healed and reconnected. They all sprang to their feet with wide-open eyes and continued patrolling, as if nothing had ever occurred.

Joshua led the band of ninjas as they walked along the dirt road. Kyle, Catherine, Michael, and Phillip filled Barry in on what they learned and experienced in the game.

Catherine and Phillip quickened their steps so they could walk alongside Joshua. Phillip spoke up and said, "We've been meaning to ask you something."

"What's that?" Joshua asked.

"What made you give up on competing in online gaming competitions?" Phillip inquired.

"Yeah, I used to watch you at home. You were the best," Catherine chimed in.

"In all honesty, most of the games became too easy. It just wasn't challenging anymore. So, I got bored," Joshua answered. "Tell me, why do you guys like video games so much?"

Catherine answered, "I have two older brothers who can be jerks sometimes. They would always play video games, but never let me join them. So, when they weren't home, I would practice, and I got so good that I kicked both their butts."

Joshua laughed. "That's cool."

"It was! I believe a girl can do anything," Catherine proudly declared.

"You know, I agree with you," Joshua said, turning his head towards Phillip.

"Well, my life is pretty much set," Phillip commented.

"What do you mean?" Joshua asked.

"My dad told me as soon as I graduate from high school, I'll be going to Harvard, his alma mater. He gave me two choices: become a doctor or a lawyer. But when I play video games, I can be anything I want. I can be a wizard, a football player, a basketball player, or even a ninja—although that didn't work out so hot here," Phillip explained.

They all burst out laughing.

Barry swiftly walked up behind them to listen to the conversation and asked, "Hey, what's so funny? What are you guys talking about?"

Joshua glanced at him. "I'll tell you later."

As they got closer to a floating sign that read "Level Thirteen", a surge of power hit them.

"Whoa, what the heck was that?" Joshua asked.

"I think we just leveled up," Barry replied.

"How can we be sure?" Catherine asked.

"Oh, that's easy. Kyle, pull out your sword and start swinging," Barry said.

Kyle unsheathed his sword and began a flurry of swings. His motions were faster and more fluid than before. Finishing his exhibition with a back flip, he sheathed his sword and exclaimed with surprise, "I've never been that fast before!"

"Let me give it a shot," Michael said as he flipped backward even higher than before. Upon landing, he unleashed a flurry of lightning-fast kicks and punches. His movements were so rapid they were impossible to see. "Woo-hoo! Yeah, baby! That's what I'm talkin' about!" Michael said with excitement.

"How did you know?" Phillip asked, looking at Barry.

"I figured it's just like any other video game. When you move to the next level, your abilities increase," Barry casually answered.

"Yeah, you level up. Makes sense. Come on, let's keep moving," Joshua said, still feeling a powerful energy surge running through him.

Walking towards a white marble bridge, they saw two lion statues on both sides, with water streaming from their mouths into the river below. They felt a sense of wonder as they looked up and saw the distant horizon, where the sky was engulfed in a mesmerizing bluish-white glow.

Joshua carefully approached the edge of the bridge, raising his hand to warn the group. "Don't come any farther," he said.

"This is a puzzle, right?" Kyle asked.

"Yes, it is, but we must complete it in perfect synchronicity for it to work," Joshua explained.

"What will happen if we just try to cross?" Michael asked.

"Do you really want to know?" Joshua asked.

"Yeah, sure," they all answered.

Joshua warned, "Stand back" as he picked up a stone from the ground. All the kids complied and stood back.

Joshua tossed a stone onto the bridge. Suddenly, the lions sprang to life and pounced onto the bridge, roaring ferociously, glaring at them with pointed teeth and visibly sharp claws. The group stayed silent and motionless. After a few moments, the lions climbed back up on their perches, assumed their previous positions, and transformed back into stone, with water spewing out of their mouths just as before.

Michael glanced at Joshua and remarked, "Yo, man, you got problems."

Confident, Phillip walked up to Joshua and said, "I think I know how to solve it."

"Okay, tell me how?"

"It's obvious that no player could cross the bridge and face that many beasts," Phillip stated cleverly.

"Correct. And what else?" Joshua asked, smirking.

"The player would need to use a projectile to hit the lions in the correct order and pass," Philip answered.

"Very good, but in what order? I'll give you a hint. The answer is right in front of you," Joshua said smugly, folding his arms.

They all looked around for clues except Catherine, who was busy munching on an apple she had hidden in her gi. After a minute of not being able to solve the puzzle, they all shrugged and shook their heads.

"Where is it, Uncle Josh?"

"Let me show you," Joshua said, picking up two stones. He then explained, "This level provides a solution for players without arrows or shuriken. They can use these instead."

Joshua threw a stone at the lion statue on the right, making it spin and spray water on the walkway, turning the marble green. Then, he hurled a second stone at the left lion, causing it to spin and spray yellow water onto the bridge. The yellow water mixed with the green water, turning the marble walkway blue, mirroring the horizon. All the lions' mouths closed.

"We can pass now," Joshua proudly declared, leisurely strolling across the bridge. The children trailed behind him, stealing glances at the lions, fearing that they might awaken before they reached the other side.

As they followed down another path. "What now?" Catherine asked, mindful of every step.

"Relax. There are no traps in this area," Joshua said.

"Then where?" Phillip asked in relief.

"Up ahead. We're almost there," Joshua answered.

After traversing half a mile, they approached the edge of a deep, black canyon, where a ten-foot clearing awaited.

All eyes turned to Joshua.

"Can't we just jump across to the other side with our ninja abilities?" Michael asked.

"I wouldn't do that if I were you," Joshua cautioned.

"Why not?" Barry asked.

"The rock face on the other side is as smooth as glass, so even if the player jumped across and tried to use the shuko to grip onto something, they couldn't," Joshua explained.

"And what's down there?" Catherine asked with a sense of dread in her voice, her gaze fixed on the ominous void, her ears filled with the unsettling noises of clicking, slithering, and slurping echoing from the depths.

"Trust me. You don't wanna know," Joshua answered.

"Man, you must have had a terrible childhood or something," Michael said, shaking his head. He also looked down at the foreboding dark crevasse and imagined the myriad of nightmarish traps that Joshua had devised in the game. "How do we get across then?" he asked.

Joshua picked up a large conch shell from the ground and blew into it to solve the puzzle. The sound of the conch shell resembled that of a foghorn, and it reverberated throughout the wind-swept canyons. Suddenly, a multitude of colorful cobblestones emerged from the canyon and formed a raised pathway that extended from one side to the other.

"In order to discover the secret to crossing the Abyss of Doom, the player would need to have purchased a map on

Level Five that has the secret written on the bottom," Joshua explained.

"So, if a player didn't buy the map on Level Five, or couldn't figure it out, they would have died or remained stuck here forever?" Phillip asked in shocking revelation.

"Yup. Most likely die though," Joshua answered. He paused for a moment, reflecting on his words, realizing they weren't very encouraging for the young teens. A wave of regret and shame washed over him as he remembered Lin's words: "*What might be easy for you might also be difficult for others.*" He lowered his head and apologized. "Sorry, guys. I put too many tough challenges into the game."

The kids all nodded, accepting his apology.

"So how do we do this?" Michael asked.

"Let's just get across. I wanna go home!" Kyle said, raising one foot, preparing to step on a stone.

Joshua swiftly yanked Kyle away from the hovering stone path. "The map gave instructions on the correct pattern for the player to use when crossing. If not done precisely, the pathway will collapse."

"Ah, come on!" Catherine said in frustration.

"Everyone be quiet and listen carefully," Joshua said. "Follow the pattern of two feet down on the purple stones, hop with the left foot onto a white stone, hop to a black stone with the right foot, and then hop onto the green stones, landing with both feet and walking across." Joshua prepared himself and said, "I'll go first."

"Good idea," Philip said.

"Uncle Josh, be careful."

Joshua cautiously hopped onto the purple stones, relieved to see the levitated path holding steady. He then jumped onto the white stone landing with his left foot, then hopped onto the black stone with his right foot, before leaping onto the green stones with both feet and walking to the landing, where he sighed in relief.

He shouted across to them, "It's safe, guys. Come on. Remember, it's both feet on purple, left foot on white, right foot on black, and both feet on green!"

"Hopscotch from hell," Michael muttered nervously as he went next.

As Michael carefully made his way across, Barry leaned into Phillip's ear, whispering, "Are you sure we can trust Joshua?"

"What are you talking about? He's the one who got us this far," Phillip answered dismissively.

"Yeah, but think about it. He's the one who created this game with all these deadly traps," Barry said, trying to pique suspicion.

"You just got here. You really don't have a clue about what you're talking about," Catherine said defensively. "He's our friend."

One by one, they tactfully crossed the abyss of doom to safety on the other side.

As they continued walking, the mouthwatering smell of baked bread permeated the air.

"You smell that?" Catherine asked, sniffing the air.

"Yeah, I do," Kyle answered.

"Look, there's a village over there?" Michael pointed to a nearby marketplace.

"With our gold, maybe we can buy new weapons and food there," Philip said.

"Sorry, can't do that, guys," Joshua said, bursting their bubble.

"Why not?" Barry asked.

"Because ninjas are outlawed assassins. So, unless any of you have a change of clothes, the moment we enter that village, over fifty samurai guards will attack us," Joshua explained.

"Damn! Now we have to go back to stealing food from carts." Michael said, shaking his head in disappointment.

"No, hold your horses. Further up the road, there is a merchant and caravan where we can purchase weapons and food. But you can only spend two gold coins each for your purchases," Joshua said.

"But I don't have any gold," Barry reminded them.

"Don't worry about it. We'll share with you," Joshua answered.

"Why only two?" Philip inquired.

"The excessive weight," Joshua revealed, looking at their confused faces, then continued. "I set a trap that would trigger if a player had more than five pieces of gold and was carrying weapons. It would cause the cobblestone path to collapse, sending the player plummeting to a horrifying death."

Joshua's explanation of the secret to the abyss of doom shocked the kids. Kyle was the only one who didn't seem concerned. Everyone exchanged worried looks and watched Joshua as he walked away. Kyle left and followed his uncle, while the other kids glanced at each other before hesitantly traipsing after them.

The group walked another mile along the trail until they came across a horse-drawn cart where an elderly man with silver hair and a long white beard presented them with various items and delicacies to purchase. They bought new weapons and fresh food from the merchant and continued on their journey.

# CHAPTER 19

# RACE FURY

In the game Race Fury, Zachary, a thirteen-year-old male, Caucasian teenager, skillfully maneuvered his red and white McLaren MP4/4 along a serpentine racetrack, while many other vehicles zoomed by, some colliding with his door and rear bumper.

"That's right, racing fans! This is Level Fourteen and only one more lap to go to be the winner!" the announcer's voice said, sounding like a carnie barking over the arena speakers.

Zachary made a pit stop, where men in white jumpsuits and dark sunglasses changed the McLaren MP4/4's tires and refueled his car.

"Help me, please. I can't do this anymore!" Zachary screamed and attempted to climb out of the Formula 1 race car, but felt as if he was bolted to the seat. "How can I get home?" Zachary tearfully asked.

The man methodically attended to his vehicle, ignoring his desperate pleas for help.

They lowered the car off the jacks. One man gave him the thumbs up, shouting, "Go! Go! Go!"

Zachary raced off to complete his last lap, expertly passing cars and staying on the apex of the turns. In the distance, he spotted two buxom blonde women on either side of the speedway, each waving a checkered flag. So, he pressed the accelerator to the floor and zoomed past the front car, crossing the finish line. The blonde bombshells waved the checkered flags, signifying the winner.

"And our winner of Level Fourteen is car number forty-two! Zachary Wilson!" the announcer blared.

The computer-generated crowd applauded and cheered as he pulled to the side of the track, surrounded by reporters and camera flashes. He parked the McLaren. To his utter surprise, he realized he could climb out of the car. His legs were limp and sore, and his jumpsuit was stained with urine from being trapped inside the car for two extended difficult levels of the game. He pulled off his helmet, feeling a sense of relief.

The two blondes, speaking in perfect unison, eagerly embraced him and said, "Congratulations, winner."

"I made it to Level Fifteen. How do I get out of here?" Zachary asked the two women.

"Congratulations, winner!" the women repeated.

"I said, How do I get out of here?" Zachary demanded again in frustration.

"Congratulations, winner," the two women reiterated, sounding like a recording.

A bright yellow Ferrari SF70H pulled up alongside Zachary, catching his attention as its engine roared. Zachary turned to face the source of the noise. The Game Master, dressed in a sleek yellow and black racing suit, stopped his car and lifted the visor on his helmet, revealing his piercing gold eyes. "Hello, Zach," he said, greeting Zachary with a chilling wave.

"I made it to Level Fifteen. Can I go home now?" Zachary asked desperately.

"Not yet. You still must defeat me, the Boss Racer. If you can do that, then you can go home," The Game Master replied.

Zachary hung his head in exhaustion, then lifted it, saying with bravery, "Let's go, if that's what it takes to get home."

"That's the spirit! What kind of car do you want to race me in?" The Game Master asked.

Zachary thought for a moment. "I'll take the Mercedes W11."

"Oh, excellent choice," The Game Master said, rubbing his hands together in delight.

On the starting line, a self-driving blue Mercedes W11 pulled up next to The Game Master's Ferrari.

Zachary put on his helmet again, pulled down the visor, and climbed inside.

"Let me give you the rules of this race. It's only ten laps; the first to the finish line is the winner; second place is the loser. The winner gets a medal. The loser dies," The Game Master sneered, unsettling Zachary.

"Gentlemen, start your engines!" the announcer's voice came over the loudspeakers.

The Game Master and Zachary revved their engines, filling the air with a thunderous rumble and the pungent smell of fuel. Zachary gripped the steering wheel, glancing up at the red light above him, his heart racing.

"Three, two, one! Go!" the announcer roared, and the light turned green.

Zachary and the Game Master flew down the track, their screeching tires leaving marks on the asphalt. Lap after lap, the two competitors remained neck and neck in the race. The Game Master narrowly surpassed Zachary, who then sped up and passed him on a turn. In a fit of anger, the Game Master aggressively crashed into Zachary's Mercedes W11, laughing mockingly and giving him the finger. Zachary, seething with rage, shifted to the side and dabbed his brake, enabling The Game Master to take the lead. He then shifted into fourth gear and sped up, ramming into the back of The Game Master's car.

The Game Master looked out his rear-view mirror and shouted, "Hey, what are you doing!?"

"I'm freaking tired of you. I said I want to go home!" Zachary screamed, smashing into the back of The Game Master's car, sending it spinning out of control and into the firewall. Zachary pulled ahead and cast a glance over his shoulder at the crash scene. He smiled.

"One more lap will determine the winner of this race," the announcer's voice blared.

In the distance, a dimensional door materialized beside the finish line, glowing in a bluish-white hue. Seeing the door, the Game Master became incensed. He regenerated his car and put it in reverse, muttering, "Oh no, you don't. You runt, nobody beats me!"

The Game Master straightened his car on the racetrack and took off at top speed towards Zachary.

Zachary could see his bedroom silhouette through the dimensional gateway as he neared the finish line. Filled with a sense of victory, he shouted, "I'm going home. Yes! I'm going home!" as he got closer to the rift.

The Game Master pulled up next to him. Seeing his car, Zachary rapidly pressed the accelerator to the floor, shifting gears to pass The Game Master.

The Game Master eagerly opened a small box on his dashboard and yelled, "Nitrous oxide! Loser! Woo-hoo!" pressed a red button, and his Ferrari SF 70H zoomed past Zachary's car in a yellow blur, passing the finish line.

"The winner and still champion of boss Level Fifteen is none other than The Game Master!" the announcer's voice thundered over the loudspeakers.

As cheers filled the air, the dimensional doorway vanished. The two blondes rushed over to congratulate the winner as he climbed out of his car.

Zachary's spirits sank into hopelessness as he watched the door disappear. He realized he was stuck in a never-ending race he could never win. The Game Master would keep cheating to ensure that. As tears rolled down his face, he closed his eyes and slammed on the brakes at full speed, causing his car to flip over and burst into flames.

In the empty employee lounge of a famous auto body and tire shop, the TV flickered erratically. The screen shattered and spewed out Zachary's charred body onto the floor.

# CHAPTER 20

# GOING ACCORDING TO PLAN

In Geneva, Switzerland, the following day, Dr. Zarius sat at a mahogany desk in his study, browsing through an international news app on his laptop. An article recounting the shocking and unexplained death of a teenage girl from America captured his attention. Authorities found the upper torso of the victim in the sea-soaked living room of her Virginia residence. The corners of Dr. Zarius' thin lips subtly curled into a smile. He continued scrolling through the news, looking for similar stories. He came across another article about the gruesome death of a teenage boy found in his Wisconsin home wearing boxing gloves and shorts. Someone pulverized the boy's head and jaw. He continued searching and, once again, saw an article recounting the bizarre death of another teenage boy. The boy was found wearing a ninja costume with two arrows lodged in his back. Police discovered the boy's body in the basement of his uncle's home in Vancouver, Canada.

A sinister smirk appeared on Dr. Zarius' face, and in his excitement, the cottage trembled. Wanting a better look at the scenes that were unfolding, Dr. Zarius stood up and walked over to his fireplace. The flames grew taller and hotter, and from the burning embers, an image took shape. Dr. Zarius gazed into the fire—face aglow—and saw Zachary's charred body and skull lying dead on the floor of an empty auto body shop. He stared at the scene until he was satisfied and waved his hand over the flames before returning to his seat. The fire calmed to a steady burn.

# CHAPTER 21

# THE BROTHERS OF POISON

In the game world of Ninja Killers, Joshua, Kyle, Philip, Michael, Catherine, and Barry felt a surge of power as they ventured into Level Fourteen, The Land of Forever Night. A swamp with trees so dense that the sun's rays never broke through. Joshua lifted his hand to signal a halt, then picked up a samurai sword and three arrows from a tree stump. He stared strangely at the blood-stained arrow tips.

"At least we know what happened to Felicia and Joseph," Catherine said with sadness.

After exchanging worried glances with one another, Joshua carefully put the weapons back where he found them. Seeing how tired the group was, he said, "Let's take a breather, guys."

They settled themselves on the plush green grass, gathering near a towering tree in a secluded spot where the moonlight filtered in.

"What's up ahead?" Phillip asked.

"The brothers of poison."

"Who are they, Uncle Josh?" Kyle asked, stretching his back.

"They are three ninjas who guard the cave of Budan, the pirate king," Joshua replied.

"Who's that?" Michael asked, cracking his knuckles.

"Budan is a Level Twenty samurai mini-boss. He's extremely fast and powerful and uses a broad spear as a weapon," Joshua answered.

"Will we be able to get past them?" Catherine asked, a worried expression crossed her face.

"Actually," Joshua explained, "there's a secret path that leads around the swamp. We'll take that route to avoid them."

Confused, Kyle looked at Joshua. "Uncle Josh, why are the three ninjas called 'The Brothers of Poison,' and what is their connection to Budan?"

"Do you all want to hear the backstory of Budan and the brothers of poison?" Joshua asked.

They nodded their heads yes.

Joshua positioned himself in the middle of the circle of kids and, as the moonlight cast a shadow on his face, he began the tale. "Once, long ago, there was a beautiful woman, Mira, who fell in love with a soldier, Hoshi. They got married. Not too long afterwards, Mira gave birth to triplet boys, Haru, Akio and Goro. They were extremely happy, but one day Hoshi was sent off to war and enemy soldiers killed him on the first day of battle."

"That's so sad," Catherine remarked.

"Yes, it was. The boys' mother did her best to raise her three sons on her own, but it was just too hard. She made the tough choice to send her sons to an orphanage. When they were only six years old, Budan adopted the three boys."

"Why did he do that?" Michael asked.

"Budan trusted none of his fellow pirates around his precious gold. He thought it best to adopt the three boys and have the ninja clans train them in the ways of the ninja, so when they grew up, he would have their complete allegiance."

"Budan sounds like a straight hustler to me," Michael said, grinning.

Joshua chuckled and then continued the story. "He made a deal with the leader of the ninja clan to train them in martial arts and give them a special ability. They would train rigorously for hours each day and then take a small amount of poison, gradually building up immunity."

"Why on earth would they do that?" Phillip asked, confused.

"So, they can easily poison their victims and not be affected. The brother's saliva or sweat can be used on their weapons. One cut, even the slightest nick from one of their weapons, would instantly kill their opponent. Each of the brothers was given specially crafted weapons to wield according to their skill. Haru was given a sword; Akio, a bow; and Goro, who was a fighter, was given boots with retractable blades," Joshua explained.

"You're right, they seem dangerous," Barry said, appearing nervous.

"They are. They will guard Budan and his gold with their lives. That's why we're going to use the secret passageway to avoid an unnecessary fight and get to Level Fifteen," Joshua said, assuring them.

"Good idea, Uncle Josh," Kyle said, yawning.

"The best ever," Catherine said, laying her head on a burlap sack to sleep.

"All of you get some rest. I'll stay on guard. We still have ways to go," Joshua said, wanting to rest but deciding not to. Remembering the blood-stained arrow tips, he worried if they could pull it off without someone getting hurt or worse. He glanced around at the now-sleeping kids and kept watch.

# CHAPTER 22

# BETRAYAL AND BUDAN

Hours later, Joshua woke the kids, who stood on their feet, stretching and yawning. Joshua pulled up his cowl, covering the lower half of his face, and said, "As soon as we leave this area, we must be completely silent. No talking. The secret passageway is near the edge of the swamp, but any noise will alert the brothers of poison. Are we clear?"

They all nodded and pulled up their cowls.

Like six black cats, they silently made their way through the dark, crouching and crawling amidst the towering, wet rice plants. As they got closer to the swamp, all they could hear were crickets and toads. Joshua signaled with his hand, and they all stopped. He gestured to the right and crouched down even lower. They followed his movements.

About twenty feet from the swamp's edge, Joshua revealed a narrow, hidden passage by pulling back some brush.

"I didn't know that was there!" Barry shouted.

"Shhh! Shut the hell up, man! Didn't you hear what Josh said?" Michael whispered, glaring angrily at Barry.

"Yeah, I heard him just fine. I have just one thing to say." Barry then pointed at them and yelled, "Over here! Come out! Come out! The intruders are here!"

Joshua, alarmed by Barry's actions, grabbed him by the shoulders. "Why? What are you doing?"

"The Game Master promised me I could rule Level Eleven in this world. In the real world, I'm nothing, but here I live like a king! I tried to warn you, like those other kids, but just like them, you wouldn't listen. Oh, well, sucks to be you!" Barry chuckled, running away through the marsh.

"Bastard!" Catherine huffed, placing an arrow on her bowstring and aiming at Barry's back. But the arrow missed him and got lodged in a tree.

"Who dares to steal the gold of the mighty Budan!" a loud, gruff voice sounded from the swamp.

They turned around to find an intimidating samurai, as big as a sumo wrestler, adorned in bronze, metallic armor, holding a broad spear. Haru jumped out of a bamboo tree with his sword. Goro crawled out of the water, and Akio walked from behind a large boulder holding his bow.

"I will allow you filthy pigs to retreat. If you choose to fight, you must defeat my sons, then face me. Whichever choice you make, your ultimate fate is a brutal and agonizing death!" Budan shouted menacingly.

The brothers of poison stood next to him, their eyes aglow in a vibrant emerald green, piercing through the darkness as they stared at Joshua and the kids.

"I guess that's them. Why do their eyes look like that?" Phillip asked, his voice trembling.

"It's an effect of the poison. There's no going back now," Joshua replied.

"Why not, Uncle Josh?" Kyle asked, swallowing hard.

"As soon as we turn our backs, Akio will strike us down with his arrows," Joshua answered, stealing a quick glance at the kids.

"This is too damn much." Michael shook his head.

"Alright, here's the plan. We spread out. Michael, you and I will take out Goro, since he's the strongest of the three. Phillip and Catherine, your target is Akio. Kyle, you'll have to handle Haru until help arrives. Take my sword," Joshua said, handing his weapon to Kyle, and added, "Its striking power is stronger than the one you have. Your fighting skills should be a match for his. And remember, guys, don't let any of their weapons touch you."

They all nodded in understanding.

"Let's go!" Joshua shouted.

Budan tapped the hilt of his spear on the ground, yelling, "Attack! Attack my ninjas! Kill them all!"

Prepared for battle, Joshua, Kyle, Michael, Phillip, and Catherine ran towards the charging brothers of poison.

Joshua and Michael flipped high in the air and landed in front of Goro, who instantaneously launched a front leg kick towards Joshua. Goro's boots, armed with deadly blades, dripped poison onto the rice stalks, causing them to wither. Michael struck Goro's head with several quick jabs. Goro tried a backflip and spinning wheel kick at Michael, but Michael evaded it while Joshua struck Goro's face with an open-handed palm strike.

Goro was struggling to take on two opponents at once, and Akio took notice. Akio licked the metal tip of his arrow to lace it with poison and nocked it on his bow. As he prepared to shoot Joshua, an arrow skimmed past his head, missing him. He turned his head and saw Catherine preparing to shoot another arrow his way, so he quickly sent one of his own flying directly towards her head. With masterful skill, Phillip threw a shuriken and deflected the arrow, altering its trajectory.

Kyle and Haru engaged in a fierce battle, expertly blocking and parrying each other's clashing swords. Haru thrust his sword forward, causing Kyle to jump back and almost lose his footing.

Phillip threw a shuriken at Haru, who sensed the incoming projectile, and leaped out of harm's way. The shuriken nearly missed Kyle, who shouted at him, "Hey! Be careful with those things!"

"Sorry!" Phillip yelled, hurling several more shuriken at Haru, who kept effortlessly dodging each one with a series of impressive backflips.

Catherine and Akio inched towards each other, rapidly firing arrows that collided and splintered in midair. Catherine reached into her quiver only to find it empty. "Oh no," she said with great alarm.

As Akio aimed his poison arrow towards her chest, she clenched her eyes shut in fear. Right as he was about to release his bowstring, a razor-sharp shuriken pierced his hand, making him lose his grip on the bow. Catherine opened her eyes in relief, watching as Phillip flipped onto Akio's back and slit Akio's throat with the serrated edge of the shuriken that he held in his hand like a knife. Carotid blood spurted from Akio's neck as he dropped limp onto the ground.

Catherine shouted at Phillip, "I'm out of arrows! Go help the others!" Phillip nodded and took off running.

Joshua was gaining the upper hand on Goro as he relentlessly struck the brother of poison on the back of the head. In a fit of rage, Goro delivered a powerful, lightning-quick strike with his back fist, hitting Joshua and causing him to lose consciousness. Then, he targeted Michael, unleashing a flawless series of front kicks and crescent kicks that Michael evaded. Michael glimpsed Joshua lying on the ground and, in doing so, he narrowly avoided a punch to his own face.

"Help! Somebody, help!" Michael yelled.

Phillip reached into his gi for a shuriken but came up empty-handed. He scurried through the grass on his hands and knees, searching for a much-needed projectile. A sense of dread fell upon him as he looked up to see Haru descending on him with his sword. Phillip closed his eyes.

The clanging sound of Kyle's sword blocking Haru's blade caused Phillip to reopen them. Phillip quickly wrapped his arms around Haru in a tight bear hug while Kyle plunged his sword into Haru's chest. He collapsed to the ground, his hand firmly clenching his sword.

Joshua regained consciousness and heard Michael's desperate pleas for help. He sprang to his feet and dashed behind Goro, putting him in a headlock.

"Grab his legs!" Joshua shouted to Michael. Reacting swiftly, Michael dodged Goro's kick, grabbing his knees and holding on tight.

With great strength, Joshua started rotating Goro's head in a counterclockwise motion, making sure not to touch his bare skin. Goro's neck broke with a loud snapping sound. Joshua and Michael dropped Goro's flailing body as it fell to the ground.

Filled with anger, Budan furiously placed a large samurai helmet on his enormous head and exclaimed, "You have killed my sons, now you will die!" Budan sprinted towards them with the ferocity of a wild rhino.

"How do we stop this guy?" Phillip asked as they backed away.

"His armor is virtually impenetrable. The eye opening in his helmet is his only weak spot and—" Before Joshua could complete his sentence, Budan threw his spear towards the group; it sliced through the air with the speed and power of a tornado, blowing them backwards.

Kyle, Michael, Joshua, and Catherine evaded Budan's spear and sprang up from the ground, regaining their balance. Budan leaped in front of them. Catherine stepped back as the others began kicking and punching at his sturdy armor.

As Catherine helplessly watched the battle, an idea struck her, compelling her to run away.

Phillip stayed determined amidst the chaos, crawling on the ground in search of a shuriken to help his friends in the battle.

Budan front-kicked Michael, propelling his body through the air, landing near Phillip. Phillip stopped his search and rushed towards Michael to help him get back on his feet.

Kyle jumped onto Budan's back, trying to force his sword through the narrow slits of his helmet with no success. Budan flung Kyle off, as if he were tossing a rag doll, sending him soaring in the air and crashing to the ground.

"Kyle!" Joshua yelled and grabbed one of Budan's massive arms, trying to restrain him.

Budan menacingly laughed at Joshua's attempt to hold him and picked Joshua up by his throat. Kyle sprang to his feet and joined Phillip and Michael in attacking Budan. They pounded away at his armor with their weapons and hands, trying to weaken him. Budan laughed at them, unscathed, still holding Joshua by the neck as he struggled to break free.

Catherine arrived at the place where Joseph and Felicia fought their last battle. Stooping to the ground, she gathered up Felicia's arrows and took off, running back across the rice field.

Budan tightened his grip around Joshua's neck as he aggressively pressed the tip of the spear against Joshua's chest, snarling, "I'm going to skewer you like a wild boar and make sure everyone watches. Slaves bring a high price on the black market. Perhaps that will be their fate."

Right before Budan could impale Joshua with his spear, an arrow whizzed through the air, finding its mark in Budan's right eye. Budan screamed in pain and released Joshua, who dropped to the ground and rolled out of the way.

Budan began tugging at the arrow lodged in his eye, still crying out in agony. Catherine nocked another arrow onto her bow and narrowed her eyes at the target as she pulled the string back to its maximum tensile strength. She silenced her thoughts, steadying herself, and whispered, "This is for Felicia, Joseph, and everyone else."

She released the bowstring. With the speed of a lightning bolt, the arrow traveled through the air and struck Budan directly in the left eye. With a savage, bestial scream, he dropped to his knees and collapsed forward, driving the arrows deeper into his skull.

"Yeah, take that, ya big lummox!" Phillip exclaimed triumphantly, pumping his fist in the air.

Catherine rushed towards them, greeted by hugs from Kyle, Phillip, and Michael, who enthusiastically said aloud, "Girl, you ain't no joke!"

"Guys, it's no time to celebrate. We have to go," Joshua said, looking warily around.

"Where to?" Catherine asked Joshua, who quickly responded, "To Budan's cave, now!"

With great urgency, they trudged through the murky swamp water until they reached a small cave hewn out of a recess. "In there," Joshua said as he entered first, the others following behind him.

# CHAPTER 23

# A TRAGIC LOSS

B udan had littered his cave with shiny gold coins, trea-
sure chests, tapestries, booty, and plunder that he
had amassed from his treacherous journeys across the vast
oceans.

Joshua pointed to a large wooden chest. "Kyle, open that.
It contains the most powerful sword in the game."

Kyle opened the chest and pulled out a glistening, ornate
samurai sword.

"Michael, look behind that picture and grab those brass
knuckles. They have the power to knock out any opponent."
Joshua then pointed his finger at a blue metal case, saying
to Phillip, "Inside are over fifty silver shuriken that can slice
through anything or anyone."

He then instructed Catherine to look through the vanity,
telling her, "Inside, you'll find a bow made of onyx and
arrows fashioned from dragon bones. Take them."

She pulled out a shiny black metallic bow and a quiver of sharp-tipped white arrows and placed them over her shoulder, dropping her old bow onto the floor.

"Everyone, fill your pockets with gold and let's get out of here," Joshua insisted.

"What do we need the gold for?" Catherine asked, stuffing gold coins into her gi along with the others.

"The ferryman," Joshua answered.

"The ferry who?" Michael asked.

"No more talk. Let's go!" Joshua ordered.

They all exited Budan's cave.

"This way," Joshua directed, walking toward a clearing in the back of the cave, where the neon words "Level Fifteen" hung in midair.

Little did they know, Akio had respawned and was hiding in a tall bamboo tree near the sign. As they neared the exit, a solitary arrow pierced through the air, its target set on Joshua. Hearing a faint rustling from above, Phillip jumped in front of Joshua.

"Aargh! Aargh!" Phillip screamed as an arrow tore through him, entering his stomach and emerging from his back. He fell to the ground, holding his belly.

In shock, they all gazed down at Phillip and then up at Akio's green eyes in the bamboo tree. Catherine swiftly fired the enhanced white arrow at Akio, splitting him in half. Akio's severed top and lower torso fell to the ground, where it lay motionless.

"Oh, no, no," Joshua said, stooping over Phillip and asking in desperation, "Why did you do that? Why?"

"I knew you were our only chance," Phillip answered in a weak voice, coughing up viscous red and green blood.

Michael kneeled next to Phillip, trembling. He pleaded, "Yo man, get up. You can't die on me. We gotta get back home. Come on, man."

"I can't feel my legs. I'm so scared," Phillip cried.

Catherine, now sobbing, looked on hopelessly at Phillip, as did Kyle and Joshua.

"Yo, man, I'm sorry for yelling at you like that. I didn't mean it," Michael said, tearing, gazing sadly down at him.

"It's okay, Michael," Phillip said, feeling his life ebb away.

"We still boys, right?" Michael asked.

Phillip grasped his hand and replied, "Still boys."

Phillip's breathing became labored as his chest heaved. He turned his head to the side and said, "Tell my mom and dad I love them," before taking his last breath.

Michael could feel his hand turn cold just before Phillip's body disappeared into thin air. He stood up, wiped his tears, and started marching back toward the swamp.

"Michael, where are you going?" Joshua asked.

Pausing, Michael glanced over his shoulder. With a clenched jaw and vengeance in his voice, he declared, "I'm going after that Barry kid. I'm gonna find him and break every bone in his body. Then, when he's had enough, I'll kill him."

Michael continued walking.

"Michael, stop!" Joshua shouted desperately. "The others have respawned as well by now. You won't be able to make it twenty yards on your own."

Michael ignored him and persisted, refusing to listen.

"Please, Michael, come back with us, please!" Catherine cried.

Michael stopped and turned around, tears running down his face. "Phillip told me what you guys talked about earlier. You know why I play video games? It's really rough where I'm from, man. You give someone a dirty look or say the wrong thing at the wrong time. It's over. Your birthday's end. I play video games to get away from all that." Michael paused for a moment and hung his head, trying to come to grips with what had just happened. He then raised his head and gazed at the group, asking, "Why, man? Why would Barry do us like that?"

Joshua took a moment before he answered the scared, hurting lad. "Some people will betray you in life. When you get older, you will learn this. But you can't let them destroy you. You keep going."

"Please, Michael, come with us. We need you," Catherine begged, wiping her tears. "We need all the help we can get. If you leave, more of us might die."

"Damn you, Barry!" Michael shouted at the top of his lungs. He knew she was right, and he would not survive without them.

Kyle had remained silent until now. As Michael walked back towards the group, Kyle felt he could see him for who he really was. He wasn't just some tough street kid; he was someone who had suffered and lost a lot in life. Kyle could relate. He placed a hand on Michael's shoulder and said, "Come on, man. Let's get outta here."

Joshua, Kyle, Michael, and Catherine passed through the Level Fifteen gateway, feeling the intense surge of leveling up. Only this time, there was no joyous celebration of their victory. All they felt was the weight of losing a friend.

# CHAPTER 24

# FIVE DAYS LATER

O utside the game, Chloe dragged herself to the front door. Her eyes were red and glossy, and her hair was a bit haggard. As she walked along the wooden floor, every step she took echoed through the house, reminding her of just how empty it was.

Chloe opened the door and was greeted by her father, who had a sorrowful look on his face and had brought a bottle of wine to help her calm her nerves.

"Oh, Dad," Chloe said, her face melted in appreciation. She opened her arms, and he stepped inside and hugged her, still holding the bottle of wine. Afterward, she showed him to the living room.

"Still no word?" he asked.

"Nothing," she replied. Mr. Shaw sat on the couch, and Chloe went to fetch a few wine glasses from the kitchen. "Not even a lead on where they might be," she said from the other room.

Upon her return to the living room, Mr. Shaw, in a desperate attempt to at least feign hope for her sake, said, "Well, it's the FBI working this case. If anyone can find answers, it's them."

"It's been five days since I filed the missing person report," she said.

Both understood that every second Joshua and Kyle remained missing diminished their hope for a safe return. The room fell silent, and Chloe poured them both a glass of wine.

Lin, Susan, and Gregory showed up at the office every day, their eyes weary from sleepless nights. The office was heavy with worry. Thoughts of Joshua and Kyle consumed their minds, making it hard to concentrate. They wanted to help find them, but the authorities remained tight-lipped. They turned to social media and the online gaming community for any sightings. As they scrolled through updates and comments, a hush fell over the room, with only the faint sounds of their computers and passing cars filling the air. With no new information about Joshua and Kyle's whereabouts, they sat at their desks, nervously waiting for the phone to ring.

# CHAPTER 25

# THE FERRYMAN

In the world of Ninja Killers, Joshua, Kyle, Catherine, and Michael approached a pier with saddened hearts. The sea filled the air with the aroma of salt and brine. Joshua rang a solemn, large bell placed on a wooden board.

"Why did you do that?" Catherine asked.

Joshua, feeling responsible and pained by Phillip's death, answered her in a low-spirited tone, "We need the ferryman to take us across."

They waited on the dock, observing from a distance a lone bamboo boat emerging from the fog and drawing closer. Standing at the bow of the longboat was a thin, elderly Asian man smoking a pipe, pushing his way towards them with a rod.

As the boat neared the dock, Joshua said, "I'll do the talking. Just make sure you have your gold coins in hand."

The ferryman skillfully maneuvered his boat in front of the dock as they walked to its edge.

"Evening, sir," Joshua said respectfully, bowing.

"Evening," the ferryman answered, bowing in return. "You rang my bell. Where is your destination?" he asked, taking long, hard puffs on his pipe.

"We would like to go to the Temple of Serene Battle," Joshua requested.

Upon hearing the destination, the ferryman's face showed concern as he looked around and cautioned, "Those waters are forbidden. Perhaps you would like to go to a market instead, or a..."

Joshua interrupted the ferryman, presenting a handful of gold coins, as did the rest.

"Maybe 'forbidden' was too harsh. You may come aboard," the ferryman remarked, eyeing the gold coins.

They stepped onto the ferry, each of them handing the man their gold coins, which he nestled into a large pouch. Michael, being the last to board, took one last look back at the path leading to the dock, hoping—almost expecting—to see Phillip there as if he had respawned, waving at him to wait a minute so he could catch up. However, no such miracle happened. Michael sighed and kept walking.

"Sit. Take a load off your feet. The Temple of Serene Battle is quite far," the ferryman said.

They sat on the wooden benches lining both sides of the deck. The ferryman used his long rod to reverse the boat and navigate through a fog bank. He then unfurled his sails.

The boat glided through the water as its sails filled with the night wind. Joshua, Michael, Catherine, and Kyle wore despondent expressions as they looked out at the ocean. The ferryman placed a large basket of dried fish, fruit, and nuts on the bench next to the kids for them to eat. Everyone grabbed food from the basket except Joshua, who remained seated, staring out at the sea. The kids observed Joshua's gloomy mood and shared concerned looks with one another.

"Are you okay, Uncle Josh?" Kyle asked, biting into an apricot.

"This is all my fault. I'm so stupid," Joshua answered, still gazing at the water.

"What's your fault?" Catherine asked, biting into a piece of dried fish.

"It was me who designed the game. I should have remembered Akio would be the first to respawn. I should have listened to Lin and Greg when they said Dr. Zarius's AI was too good to be true. Phillip's death is on me. All of this was my fault," Joshua said, and shamefully bowed his head.

"C'mon, man. None of that is your fault. Like you said, it's that guy Zarius who did all this," Michael said, expressing his support.

"He's right, Uncle Josh. It was you who instructed us on how to defeat the baddies."

"Without you, we couldn't have made it this far," Catherine said, nodding her head in agreement with the others. Catherine walked over to Joshua and gave him a tight hug, along with the other kids.

Joshua wrapped his arms tightly around the group and said, "Thank you, guys. I really needed that."

Catherine gave Joshua some dried fruits and fish and said, "Here. Eat and get some sleep. We'll need all our strength in the morning."

"You're right," Joshua said, biting into a fig.

Joshua felt completely drained, both mentally and physically. After eating, he stretched out on the ferry's deck and closed his eyes, hoping that when he woke up, he would be lying next to Chloe, and all of this was just some hideous nightmare. He drifted off into a deep sleep, comforted by the calming rhythm of the ocean waves.

# CHAPTER 26

# BOXING BASHERS

Although a hundred people won the sweepstakes, the game didn't affect everyone. Many never reached Level Twelve of their favorite game, finding the gameplay too challenging to defeat. But for those who did, they accepted the Game Master's proposal, unaware of the peril that awaited them.

Angelo Russo, a dark-haired fourteen-year-old boy, appeared in the game of Boxing Bashers. He stood in the corner of the ring, wearing a green robe and with black boxing gloves firmly fitted on his hands.

"Where am I?" Angelo asked, completely baffled.

Sal, his trainer, an overweight, elderly gentleman, massaged his shoulders and back.

A handsome boxing announcer dressed in a white tuxedo, red tie, and matching cummerbund walked to the center of the ring and spoke with a deep, grandiose voice into a microphone that was suspended in the air. "Welcome, ladies and gentlemen, to Boxing Bashers. In the arena tonight, we bring you the main event. A Level Twelve, ten-round boxing match, where the winner will move on to Level Thirteen and fight Masher the Magnificent!"

The entire crowd erupted in claps, cheers, and whistles.

The announcer pointed at Angelo, saying with enthusiasm, "In the left corner, our challenger. He stands 5 feet 4 inches tall and weighs 125 pounds. He has an impressive record of eleven knockouts and no losses. Let's give a round of applause to Angelo 'Lightning Bolt' Russo!"

The audience erupted in boos and jeers as Angelo stood in shock and disbelief, looking first at the announcer and then at the crowd.

The announcer shifted his attention to the opposite side of the ring. He pointed towards a well-built man, sporting a tan complexion and a crew cut. The man stood there, clenching his gloved hands together, while casting a fierce scowl in Angelo's direction.

"In the right corner, our champion, standing at 6 feet, 4 inches tall, and weighing 270lbs with fifteen knockouts, all resulting in deaths. Let's show respect for our hero, Milhelvic the Crusher!" the announcer proclaimed with reverence.

Milhelvic the Crusher raised his arms in victory as the crowd roared in adoration, jumping up and down with excitement, chanting, "Crusher! Crusher! Crusher!"

"Gentlemen, you may now come to the center of the ring," the announcer said.

Sal removed the robe from Angelo. The thin, pale-skinned kid hesitantly walked to the center of the ring with his trainer. His opponent did the same. Angelo glanced around, distressed, muttering to himself, "Uh, where am I? Is this really happening?"

Angelo stood face to chest with the musclebound, sweating Crusher, who looked down at him, growling. Frightened out of his wits, Angelo sprinted to the other side of the boxing ring, lifted one rope, jumped down from the ring, and headed towards the door in the back of the auditorium. Suddenly, an invisible force pulled him back into the center of the ring like a rubber band.

The referee stepped between them and instructed, "Okay, fellas. I want a good, clean fight. No hitting below the belt and no dirty stuff." The referee inspected both sets of their gloves, then said loudly, "Let's rock-n-roll!"

The audience went wild with excitement.

Angelo walked back to his corner in absolute fear and said, "I don't wanna fight. How do I get out of here?"

Sal slapped Vaseline on his face and said, "Okay, kid, just like we practiced. Lateral movement, side to side, throw your jab, then stick and move. But be careful; his right hook will take your head clean off."

Angelo stared at Sal with a terrifying look. "But, but I, uh..." Before Angelo could utter another word, Sal shoved a mouthpiece into his mouth and said, "Go get 'em, kid."

The sound of the bell filled the air. Angelo turned around to face his opponent, The Crusher. He pounded his gloves together, saying in a menacing tone, "This is gonna hurt."

Angelo began running around the ring in circles, screaming for dear life, "Help! Help!" as the Crusher chased him, swinging at the back of his head with thunderous punches.

The Game Master sat in the front row wearing a purple pin-striped suit with a green tie. An attractive brunette clung to his right arm in a white fur coat, and, on his left, a sexy blonde wore a black mink coat.

"I'd put my money on the Crusher with this one," the Game Master said, laughing hysterically at the spectacle.

CHAPTER 27

# TEMPLE OF SERENE BATTLE

"Get up, Uncle Josh!" Kyle said, shaking Joshua, who smiled, thinking he was in his bedroom and Kyle was waking him up.

When he opened his beleaguered eyes, four kids were looking down at him. He quickly sprang to his feet, and the harsh reality that none of this was a dream became very apparent.

"There, up ahead, the Temple of Serene Battle," the ferryman said, pointing to a small island with an enormous edifice set in the middle.

"Yeah, that's it," Joshua said with disappointment in his voice, knowing the toughest battle lay ahead.

The ferryman guided the boat close to the water's edge and stated, "I cannot go any further. There is no dock on this island."

"I understand. Thank you," Joshua said as Michael, Catherine, and Kyle hopped off the ferry into the knee-high water.

Just as Joshua was about to disembark, the ferryman spoke and said, "Sir, may I have a word with you?"

"Yes, of course," Joshua answered.

I've taken a few this far, but no one ever returns. "May I respectfully suggest you all go back now?" the ferryman warned.

"Thank you for your advice, but this is something that must be done," Joshua said, retrieving a small bag of gold coins from his gi and giving them to the ferryman, adding, "You can have these; we won't be needing them."

The ferryman took the satchel and seemed happy with Joshua's selfless act. Just as Joshua was about to leap off the boat, the ferryman stopped him and gave him something. Joshua looked at it, put it in his gi, and bowed in return. Then he jumped down into the water, making his way towards the kids who waited for him.

"Farewell, noble warrior," the ferryman said, reversing the boat and gliding away with open sails.

As the group waded through the water and arrived on the beach, their eyes were drawn to the magnificent temple that stood tall, just twenty feet away. Its roof, made of pure gold, shimmered in the sunlight, while wooden columns adorned with gold trim lined its sides.

Once they got closer to the temple, the group paused and stood at the base of the marble stairs that led up to the entrance. The kids gazed at the two imposing dragon statues that flanked the stairs, then back at Joshua with worried expressions etched on their faces. The kids were afraid of what lay ahead, but they wanted desperately to go home.

"What's in there?" Michael asked Joshua, staring up at the temple.

"Suko, the Lord of Ninjas."

"Who's that?" Catherine asked.

"He's a Level Twenty-five boss with all ninja abilities, and he fights with two swords—one in each hand. He's a martial arts master and uses smoke bombs to confuse his enemies, attacking when they can't see him," Joshua explained.

Michael looked down, shaking his head, with a nervous expression on his face. "Man, if we make it outta here," he said, "I'm joining a book club."

Joshua huddled close, speaking with empathy. "I understand. I know you guys are scared, and so am I. But the temple is our only way out. We can do this, okay?"

The kids nodded their heads, feeling encouraged.

"Now listen up. Suko's weakness is that he's just like any human and is vulnerable to any attack. Mike, use your brass knuckles. When he gets near you, you hit this guy like there's no tomorrow."

Michael pulled the brass knuckles out of his gi and slipped them on his fingers, asserting resolutely, "You bet I will."

"Catherine, when he throws a smoke bomb, don't shoot an arrow till the smoke clears. When you hit him, he will stagger for a few seconds, then throw his spear at you. Always move to your left when he throws his spear, understood?"

"Got it," Catherine replied, gripping her bow tightly.

"Kyle, when he comes after either of us, you strike him only twice, then backflip out of the way. He will throw a shuriken at you. Don't be there when he does," Joshua instructed, eyeing him directly.

Kyle unsheathed his sword and said, "Got it, Uncle Josh."

Joshua paused and thought for a moment, calculating all the attacks and moves he and his team had given the boss, Lord Suko, in the game. He then said bravely, looking at the kids, "We can do this. Are you guys ready?"

They answered in unison, "Ready."

Joshua walked up the long marble stairs with the kids close behind him. They arrived at a large door made of pure jade and trimmed in gold. Joshua put one hand on the door, took a breath, gathered his nerve, and pushed it open. He stepped inside with the kids in tow. Automatically, the door closed and locked.

The Temple of Serene Battle was a splendor for the eye to behold. The room's interior was vast, with wooden floors and fierce temple guardian statues positioned near large stone columns that supported planks in the ceiling above. These planks led to a small hidden alcove tucked out of sight. Decorative art adorned the walls of the room, and two large vases sat on opposite sides. Lit candles on shelves illuminated the room, adding to its beauty and showcasing exquisite calligraphy.

They stealthily walked in, their weapons ready, courageously awaiting their final and most deadly challenge. Joshua motioned with his hand for them to wait as he headed to the front of the room, where a jade-green throne sat on a black marble pedestal. He carefully scanned the room, waiting for the dreaded Lord Suko to make his entrance.

"Something's wrong," he said, recalling when the game was designed. Lord Suko should have thrown a smoke bomb and materialized, warning the player of their perilous fate. Joshua continued scanning around the room, appearing perplexed. He glanced down at his watch, noticing that it had stopped ticking, then back at the kids and shrugged.

A cloud of smoke erupted in front of the throne. Joshua swiftly back-flipped away. Catherine placed an arrow on her bow, Kyle raised his sword high in the air, and Michael got into a boxing stance, brandishing his brass knuckles. All of them stood ready for battle.

The smoke cleared, revealing The Game Master himself. He snickered and said, "Ta-da! Wasn't what you were expecting, huh?"

In a fit of rage, Joshua marched toward the small, four-foot-tall creature and demanded, "Why are you doing this? Send us home now!"

The Game Master sat on Lord Suko's throne and calmly crossed his legs, staring intensely at Joshua. "It was you, Joshua Peters, who created me."

"Huh? What are you talking about?" Joshua asked, looking dumbfounded, stepping back from the creature and standing protectively in front of the kids.

The Game Master responded with a smirk, saying, "Oh, yes. It was you. You wanted to create the ultimate gaming experience. It was you who spent years obsessed with increasing the AI of a program more averse to humans." With a wicked grin, he added, "And certain parties heard you and, well, here I am."

"Parties? What parties?" Joshua asked.

The Game Master snapped his fingers. Above its mischievous little head, a video clip from the lab, showing Joshua a month earlier, said, "I'll give anything for this game to work the way I want! Anything! Anything!"

Leaning forward and pointing downwards, the Game Master spoke in an ominous voice, "I repeat, certain parties."

"I knew it. We're in hell, man," Michael said, now terrified, his eyes darting around the room.

"Not yet, kid," The Game Master retorted, winking.

"So that's why in the lab when you were switched on, I was the only one you knew. What do you want from us?" Joshua asked, frightened, yet deeply intrigued.

"He wants our souls," Catherine said, aiming her bow at The Game Master, who looked contemptuously at her and smarmily answered, "Bingo! But you're only half right, brat." Shifting his eyes towards Joshua, he continued, "Only the blood of children can open the portal from which we can emerge into your world. And you, asshole, are the obstacle in the way."

"That's not gonna happen," Joshua stated, his fist clenched.

"Hmm, maybe, maybe not. It all depends on you," The Game Master said, uncrossing his legs.

"What do you mean?" Joshua asked.

"Here are the stakes. You beat me, and you and the rest of the little brats in the game go home. If you lose, you die, and so do they. And I will be the true Game Master. The system will go global, and the games will continue, thus opening the portal between our worlds. I will be praised by my brethren for a job well done," The Game Master proclaimed, leaning forward with a smile.

"You and your kind are not getting into our world. Not ever. Understand, piece of shit? Let's get this over with," Joshua huffed.

"Yeah, you're not killing us. You little pipsqueak," Catherine blurted out.

"Yeah, let's kick his ass!" Michael shouted, baling his fist, ready to fight for his life.

"Just say when, Uncle Josh," Kyle said, raising his sword.

The Game Master hopped down off the throne, turned around, and pulled down his trousers, mooning them. "You mean this ass?" he provocatively taunted, gesturing towards his rear end. Turning back around, he swiftly pulled up his pants, a mischievous grin spreading across his face. "Not this ass. How about this one?" He asked as his complexion transformed to a deep green hue covered with scales. His face and physique contorted into a grotesque, reptilian creature, towering at a height of ten feet. His long, razor-sharp nails resembling talons clutched an oversized battle-ax as a black and gold samurai costume adorned his muscular frame.

"What the heck?" Kyle said, awestruck, as they all stared in shock.

Catherine, her mouth agape, trembled, lowering her bow.

"There is no Lord Suko. I am now Lord Byakko, a mega-boss! Now try kicking this ass!" the creature declared in a deep, guttural voice.

Michael frantically sprinted towards the temple door, yanking on the handle to open it, screaming, "I take it back! I take it back!" but it wouldn't budge.

Joshua backed away nervously at the sight of the monstrous beast, saying, "No, you're definitely not Lord Suko."

"No, I added my own upgrade. Now it's time for you all to die," The Game Master said, glaring at them with evil black eyes.

"I don't know how this is even possible, but let's make this overgrown dinosaur extinct!" Joshua shouted to the kids.

Michael ran back to the group and stood near Joshua, ready to fight.

Just as Catherine was about to release her arrow, she, Michael, and Kyle were all paralyzed.

"I can't move, Uncle Josh!" Kyle yelled, his arm and sword raised high.

Frightened, Michael echoed, "Me neither," his brass knuckles gleaming on his clenched fist as he froze in a fighting stance.

"What is this?" Catherine asked in a panic, her arm raised, holding her bow and arrow at the ready.

"None of you chose multiplayer before entering the game. Dumbasses! This battle is between you and me, Joshua."

Joshua, still able to move, locked eyes with the horrifying creature. "A rematch. But this time, inside the game. That's what you wanted all along. You knew I'd figure it out and try to stop you."

"Yes. You beat me at the studio when we played Space Blasters. I told you then I didn't like to lose. From that moment, I knew I had to kill you in-order for our plan to succeed," Lord Byakko replied.

Joshua carefully pried the sword from Kyle's hand, exchanging his feelings of regret for the courage to end it. He stated, "It won't. Let's rock."

"Let's!" Lord Byakko roared, charging at Joshua, swinging his battle-ax.

As he got closer, Joshua flipped over the monster to avoid the kids getting hurt, then swung at it with his sword. Lord

Byakko used his ax to block Joshua's attack, then delivered a powerful kick to his chest, causing him to fly backwards and crash into the wall before sliding down to the floor.

"Yo man, be careful!" Michael yelled.

"Uncle Josh! Get up!"

Joshua leaped to his feet, reached into his gi and grabbed a handful of Phillip's shuriken, launching them at the creature. The monster deflected each one with its battle-ax. Joshua then lunged at the beast with his sword, only to be met with a fierce counterattack. Thinking quickly, Joshua tossed a smoke bomb and disappeared.

"Where are you?" Lord Byakko bellowed, sniffing the air.

Joshua hid behind one of the stone columns, hyperventilating, his heart beating out of his chest with fear. From the periphery, he watched Lord Byakko search through the temple, flipping over jars while smelling the air. Joshua crept behind the monster; his sword's tip held forward in grim determination. With a powerful leap, he pounced at Lord Byakko, who smirked and whirled around, blocking the blade. Before Joshua could react, the radiant axe cut through the air, slashing his chest, ripping his gi. Joshua back-flipped, avoiding a second fatal strike. He gritted his teeth, glancing down at the blood staining the ground at his feet. He realized the creature was far too fast and strong for him to handle.

"Oh, no!" Catherine's voice rang out.

"Uncle Josh! Remember what you told me to do when you're outnumbered, or an enemy is too strong?" Kyle shouted, watching in distress.

"He's right, think," Joshua muttered to himself. Lord Byakko rushed towards him, but before the beast could reach him, Joshua threw his final smoke bomb and vanished once more.

Waving away the smoke with his enormous hands, Lord Byakko roared, "You can't hide forever!"

Out of nowhere, Joshua jumped down from a ceiling beam and attempted to slit the monster's throat. The monster grabbed the blade and flung Joshua to the floor. As Joshua scrambled to his feet, Lord Byakko swung his battle-ax, striking him in his midsection, splitting open his abdomen.

"Josh!" the kids screamed in horror as they witnessed Joshua clutching his stomach, blood flowing out in a bright crimson stream. Casting a sorrowful gaze towards the kids, Joshua succumbed to his wounds and collapsed lifelessly to the ground.

Lord Byakko mercilessly stomped on Joshua's chest, his tremendous weight crushing him and causing his internal organs to burst, spilling out from his ruptured belly.

The kids' terrifying screams resonated throughout the temple.

# CHAPTER 28

# THE TRUE GAME MASTER

Lord Byakko raised his battleax, proclaiming, "I am The Game Master!" and began to morph back to his original size and form. He danced around the temple, laughing and shouting, "I did it! I did it!" The bells on his jester's hat jingled and swayed. He paused and glared at the kids, his face now contorting into an evil scowl.

The kids lowered their eyes as tears streamed down their faces, knowing their impending fate.

The Game Master looked down at Joshua's crushed body, rubbing his hands together, wearing a satisfied smile. He fixed his gaze back on the kids and began taunting them in a sinister tone, "Now that he's out of the way, I have an assortment of life-ending games for you brats to play. "

The kids tried to move once more, but couldn't. They desperately screamed out, "No! Please, no!"

The Game Master walked up to Kyle and started poking at his paralyzed body, trying to knock him over. Suddenly, a sword pierced him from behind and came out through his chest.

"Aargghh!" The Game Master screamed as Joshua lifted his impaled body with his sword and tossed him to the ground.

The Game Master landed on the floor, face down, with yellow blood seeping from his back.

"Josh!" the kids shouted in unison, their voices filled with a mixture of happiness and surprise as they beheld him, alive and well.

"Uncle Josh, we thought you were dead!" Kyle exclaimed with relief. Tears welled up in his eyes as he stared at his uncle in complete astonishment.

"How? I killed you. How?" The Game Master demanded, glaring at Joshua, yellow blood trickling from his mouth. He then clutched his chest and attempted to crawl away.

"What you failed to realize is that I designed the game. The only extra life and healing potion in Ninja Killers was on Level Fifteen, owned by the ferryman. And only he can decide whether to give it to the player."

"So, you—you cheated!" The Game Master yelled furiously.

"No, I used my mind," Joshua winked at Kyle.

"I hate you, hate you, you arrogant asshole," The Game Master spewed in disdain, gnashing his teeth.

"I have one last thing to say," Joshua said, following behind The Game Master, who ceased crawling upon nearing the temple door and stood up.

"And what is that?" The Game Master grunted, scowling back at him, reaching for the door handle.

"I, Joshua A. Peters, am... The Game Master!" and swiftly beheaded the Imp with one powerful swing.

The Game Master's head fell to the floor, mouth open, and let out a bloodcurdling squeal that echoed throughout the game realms, making everything shake. The characters under his control started glitching and froze. This allowed the kids to run and hide in the game's safe zones.

# CHAPTER 29

# DR. ZARIUS

D r. Zarius sat peacefully in his study, reading a book by his fireplace. He dropped the book, tilted his head back in his chair, and started screaming along with The Game Master, falling to his knees. He started scratching and tearing the skin off his skull, revealing the face of a demon with glowing red eyes underneath as two black wings unfurled from his back.

A menacing, ethereal voice thundered, "You have failed me for the last time!"

Skeletal hands shot from the wooden floor, clutching his legs and pulling him under.

"Master, I did as you commanded. I beg for your forgiveness; I should never have used an imp for such a task," he pleaded, his voice echoing as the hands relentlessly dragged him back to the inferno whence he came.

# CHAPTER 30

# GAME OVER

One by one, the trapped kids in the various games started vanishing, returning to the safety of their homes and the real world.

Robert Taylor from Texas had survived, reaching Level Fourteen in the game of War Dawgs. He stood with a group of soldiers surrounded by a swarm of enemy combatants, firing his M50 caliber weapon as the soldiers remained motionless, shouting, "Get some! Get some!" He then vanished.

In the game world of Boxing Bashers, Angelo was on his last legs and out of breath, completely exhausted from running frantically around the ring from the Crusher. After tripping and falling to the canvas, Angelo scrambled to his feet, only to be met by the powerful right hook that the Crusher was known for. Just before the punch could connect with Angelo's face, the Crusher froze.

"Uh, what?" Angelo uttered in a panting breath, looking around in confusion. His hands tingled. His body flickered in and out of existence, like a glitch, and then disappeared altogether.

Back at the studio, the building shook. "Is this an earthquake?" Gregory asked, trying to keep his balance.

"I've never heard of earthquakes in Seattle," Susan said, clinging to her desk.

"Look!" Lin shouted, pointing to the tower.

Dr. Zarius's green chip popped out of the SD slot and began levitating in the air. It then transformed into a swirling green mist and disappeared through the floor. The trio exchanged startled glances with one another, unable to comprehend what had just occurred.

In the Temple of Serene Battle, Joshua, Kyle, Michael, and Catherine winced at the Game Master's scream that reverberated throughout the temple. The kids wished they could cover their ears like Joshua. Suddenly, the Game Master's eyes grew lifeless, his mouth shut, and the noise stopped.

Catherine, Michael, and Kyle, now able to move, shouted with excitement, "You did it! You did it!" and ran towards Joshua, hugging him tightly.

"Thank you, thank you for saving us," Catherine said appreciatively, but before Joshua could speak, she disappeared.

"Josh, you the man. Thanks bro," Michael said gratefully, holding up his hand for a high five with Joshua. But before their hands could meet, Michael also vanished.

"Where did they go? What now, Uncle Josh?"

"I think we're finally going home," Joshua said with relief, smiling and looking around at the scenery that was slowly fading away, turning into darkness.

Kyle gazed down at the floor, which appeared to be crumbling, then stared up at Joshua with concern. Joshua cast a bewildered gaze at his nephew, not knowing what to do. He sputtered, "Don't... don't move."

Kyle, now frightened, nodded.

Joshua glanced around at the encroaching darkness that would soon engulf them, wondering why they were still there. The game was over, and he had won. Why hadn't they vanished like the others? Joshua desperately searched inside his ninja gi, looking for something, anything, that could help.

The ground collapsed beneath Kyle. Joshua swiftly caught him, balancing him on the intact portion of the floor on which he stood. "Uncle Josh, I'm scared. I don't wanna die," Kyle said, gasping in tears.

"Neither do I," Joshua whispered as he looked hopelessly at his nephew. "I'm sorry, buddy. I don't know what to do," he said, his voice cracking with emotion, fighting to keep his tears at bay. Joshua had already concluded that if they didn't vanish soon, they would suffocate in the empty abyss. Desperately, he glanced around one last time as the darkness closed in on them. The air grew thinner, oxygen running low. He reached out his arms to embrace Kyle, who hugged him tightly.

The remaining floor disintegrated, sending Joshua and Kyle plummeting into a terrifying, endless chasm as they screamed in horror.

# CHAPTER 31

# BACK HOME

C hloe sat across from her father on the sofa, completely distraught and overwhelmed. He attempted to calm her, but to no avail.

There was a loud thud above their heads.

"Did you hear that?" she asked.

Then another thud. Chloe and her father locked eyes. She sprang to her feet and ran up the stairs.

"Dear, hold on!" her father said, following his daughter.

Chloe flung open Kyle's bedroom door to see Joshua and Kyle, both panting and sweating, standing in the room, dressed as ninjas.

"Joshua! Kyle!" Chloe shouted.

"Chloe!" Joshua exclaimed, embracing her as they pressed their tear-stained faces against each other.

Kyle hugged them both, also crying.

Chloe asked with a mix of concern and delight, "Where have you been? I was worried sick about you two. And why are you guys dressed like that?"

Joshua and Kyle exchanged silent glances.

Joshua grabbed the Game Master System from Kyle's desk and forcefully slammed it onto the floor, stomping it into pieces.

"What in the world? Why did you do that? That was your dream!" Chloe asked, confused.

"No, no," Joshua said, shaking his head, continuing, "You and Kyle are my dream."

Joshua, Chloe, and Kyle embraced each other again, not wanting to let go.

Chloe's father stood in the bedroom doorway, bewildered, watching them cling to each other. "Can someone tell me what's going on?" he asked.

Joshua glanced at Mr. Shaw, then took a moment to explain what he could without going into too much detail.

Just minutes later, a pot-bellied man sat next to his sour-faced, slender wife in a dingy, neglected trailer home watching TV. Despite his efforts, his t-shirt couldn't hide his protruding gut as he sprawled out on a worn-out sofa with a faded flower print, enjoying a beer and smoking a cigarette.

The TV shot Barry onto the floor.

"Mom, Dad, I'm back," Barry said, happy to have survived.

"So what?" his dad huffed, standing up and saying, "You just broke our damn TV set. How dit-chu get in there any-way? Dumbass." Clutching his can of beer, he stormed out the door.

"And just when the movie was gettin good," his mother said, scowling at him, tightening a curler in her hair, puffing on her cigarette. She then quickly followed her husband outside.

Realizing that no one cared, something inside Barry snapped. He buried his head in his hands and mumbled through quiet sobs, "My life sucks. My life sucks."

The following day, Joshua shut down the Game Master Sys-tem and told his team to switch projects. He took a long break, which gave him and Kyle time to recover from the game's horrific events. These were especially traumatic for Joshua, who had died and come back to life. He and Kyle agreed to keep the supernatural events a secret.

The investigation into the missing kids ended with their safe return. Even though many of the young teens recount-ed incredible tales of being trapped in a game by a small creature and fighting for their lives. It was dismissed by the authorities for lack of evidence and deemed to be a social media prank. Yet other parents from the United States and Canada still mourned, unable to find answers about the horrifying, gruesome deaths of their own kids. Some vowed never to give up searching for the truth.

# Chapter 32

# SWITZERLAND

In Geneva, Switzerland, six months later, a black-gloved hand smashed the glass door of an abandoned cottage. The intruder surveyed the surroundings, ensuring that no one had heard the noise, and then slipped inside. In the darkness, the trespasser began searching through Dr. Zarius's study, grabbing papers from a desk and throwing books off the shelves. While moving through the room, the intruder heard a peculiar, hollow squeak beneath their feet. He kneeled down and used a penlight to examine the floor. Using a small knife retrieved from his pocket, he pried up a floorboard and uncovered a silver box. Opening it, he found a slender green chip, about the size of an SD card, and stood up, whispering, "I must know what this technology is."

Lin placed the chip in his pocket and swiftly exited the premises.

The floorboard fixed itself back into place.